Blood
Land

R.S. Guthrie

For my father,
who pined for great tales
and who loved Wyoming
as much as any pioneer.
I miss you.

ACKNOWLEDEGMENTS

First, you don't write a novel about Wyoming and not acknowledge the genuine, unique, hard-working, tough-loving people of the land itself. I have many friends there still, both American and Native American. The latter know how I feel about history, but every one of you has a pride that no one will ever be able to take away. I depict the ranchers in a way I had to for the story. I admire what you all do. There is one quote I repeat here, because it's the truest thing in rural Wyoming: *They might tolerate you, even befriend you—but it was a closed society.* I say that with the deepest respect. You are the toughest, hardest-working men and women I've ever had the pleasure of knowing.

The Bull Rider's Prayer is not mine, and I dedicate it to Eb Richie, who may not read this book but whom I did see one evening in the town drugstore years after high school and his face looked just as I described it. That night, the bull had won.

To my editor, Russell Rowland, an acclaimed, published writer in his own right: you did me a solid and, as always, you made my words better with each and every suggestion. You are also the best I know at also providing the positive "nice" where earned.

To my proofreader, Becky Illson-Skinner, you are as talented as you are lovely and no book should ever go out without coming under an eye as studious as your own.

To my main beta reader, friend, and confidant Gail Gentry—whose forthcoming novel will undoubtedly show the world yet another crazy talent from the Indie world—words don't express my gratitude for everything you've done.

To my wife, Amy, who has read *Blood Land* more times in full and in part than any other living human being, thank you for believing in me but most for believing in this book as much as I do. I love you.

To bestselling author and friend, Russell Blake. Wild man. Scary man. Great writer. Without your help, I know I would not be on the road I am now. I'm not sure how I will ever thank you. Indebted forever, mi amigo.

And to the readers. Without you, we authors are without audience. Please remember, the most profound, life-altering gift you can offer the writer you love is to tell as many avid readers as you are able. We exist and succeed only as long you bring others into the fold.

"I got a letter today,
how you reckon it read?
It said, 'Hurry, hurry,
yeah your love is dead.'
I got a letter today,
how you reckon it read?
It said, 'Hurry, hurry,
you know that gal you love is dead.'"

Eddie "Son" House,
Death Letter

Chapter 1

SHERIFF PRUETT toed the edge of the obsidian, geometric opening in the earth. Approximately four feet by two, and shallow. The big man ached all over. He'd cried, shut himself up, and cried again. His heart felt so worn down it did not beat so much as murmur; a utilitarian thing without feeling or sound. The loss consumed him, and his will would not rise—muted by a damp, negative space swallowing his physical being. Pruett was *shattered*; broken in ways he might never fix. He did not know loneliness, or at least he had no memory of it. Now this singularity encased him—an invisible, merciless force threatening to erase all he was or ever would be.

Like the victim of a holocaust.

Sorrow made the old man feel weak. Exposed to the emotional elements. But like everything else, he made room for it. A man got good at tamping emotions down—one here, one there—or at least Pruett had. The problem arose when there was no more room for packing.

And this last tragedy was far too oversized for his soul to bear. Even were his stowaway places clean and emptied, he'd still never have figured a way to subjugate this much devastation—at least not for long.

What reconciliation could stand up to a fate as twisted as this?

Pruett occupied a world now where all the songbirds had flown and only carrion remained. Elemental tasks tested him: waking, standing, breathing. He was a sheriff; how did he go forward from here? Just how did the balance sheets get equaled on all sides?

A phone rang, interrupting the late afternoon boredom of a slow Saturday at the Sublette County Sheriff Dispatch in the tiny town of

Wind River, Wyoming. Sheriff James Pruett occupied the desk and answered the call.

"Sheriff's office," Pruett said

A thin, rattlesnake drawl tickled his ear: "There's been a shooting over to the Rory McIntyre place, Sheriff. Things ain't good, you need to come fast."

The caller disconnected.

Pruett couldn't move. He tried to reconcile the words; repeated them in his mind, hoping they'd scatter, reform, and produce a different result.

They didn't.

Deputy Red Horse Baptiste was on patrol. Pruett reached for the radio, his hand trembling under the sovereignty of fear.

"Baptiste," he spoke into the mike.

First, what seemed infinite radio silence, then: "Deputy Baptiste here, over."

"Get to Rory's place, Red Horse." Pruett said. "Get there *now*."

"Yessir," Deputy Baptiste said. Pruett didn't give orders that often. When he did, his deputies knew there was no point in discussion.

"Red Horse?"

"Yeah, boss?"

"Load your shotgun."

Pruett dialed the emergency volunteers. Then he called his other two deputies at their homes. He locked the office and belted his holster; loped down the courthouse steps two at a time, his considerable girth bouncing in concert. The fringes of his vision felt blurred. He would remember later that the town seemed eerily quiet with a Saturday night so soon at hand. He would also never forget the foreboding that scampered like a river of ants up and down his spine.

The county Suburban reached ninety miles per hour before Pruett got to the dip at the edge of town, took the flattest spot, and still nearly tore the front bumper off.

He drove west of town, toward the Green River Valley, straight into the glaring, tragic beauty of the Rocky Mountain sunset. The blacktop flowed beneath him, a river of opaque charcoal, its surface pocked and crackly like old, broken skin.

There was one name playing through Pruett's mind:

Bethy.

Again and again, as if looped on reel-to-reel.

God, don't you let it be her.

Not a prayer, exactly, because he hadn't done that in damn near forty years. More of a demand.

Bethy Pruett was the nexus of Pruett's whole damned *universe*. He'd known her originally as Bethy McIntyre—back when she was the cutest little pigtailed missy in grammar school. Pruett figured he'd loved her all his life, or at least as long as memory served him.

Before Sheriff Pruett.

Before the war.

Before everything.

A shiver slid through him as easily as the point of a sharpened spear pierced warm flesh. He thought about the profound force of the inevitable.

You do not always see things in time, he thought.

Not even a sheriff.

Pruett had not paid heed to the thunderclouds gathering on the horizon of their lives. But he should have. The McIntyre feud was well over a year ongoing. Father, Rory, and his two sons, Rance and Cort, made several million dollars from the gas companies that had invaded Sublette and Teton counties; like many ranchers in the area, the trio received a fortune for the mineral rights they owned. But by the bad luck of hellfire, Rory's youngest son, Ty, got nothing. As the legalities played out, Ty owned only surface rights on his inherited parcel; an oversight by the original Will and Testament of Rory's father. The county owned all rights beneath Ty's ground, so in the end all Ty McIntyre got were ruined roads, damaged irrigation, and a further hatred of democracy.

Rory, Rance, nor Cort had any legal obligation to Ty at all. And they didn't feel any. *Luck of the draw*, they often said after whiskeys in the Cowboy Bar or across the street in the Wooden Boot.

Ty blamed them for it, as any person might, and he did so openly—to anyone who would listen. Hate was Ty's common-law partner but toward his family, well, Pruett knew that hatred burrowed even wider and deeper.

Bad blood had spilled in the local saloons half a dozen times. Fists opened flesh wounds and words opened worse. Bar patrons paid the drunken scrapes little attention. Fights between Ty and anyone else were nothing new. And folks held no particular admiration for the McIntyre family. Most figured such business was typical feuding; father versus son, brother versus brother—a few small tumors that would die off once the oxygen quit flowing to them.

But Pruett knew it would go on, and so did Bethy. She knew her family was bad cement, poured from generation to generation and mixed with hateful blood. The McIntyres were racist and old school mean. Pruett appreciated the fact that he'd cut a sweet filly from a corral full of surly, untamable stallions. And though he suspected what boiled down deep, he chose to ignore it. Some of his reasons were out of respect for his wife; she was sweet-hearted to a fault and still loved all of them—naive love from the innocent, offered unrequited to cantankerous, oily hearts.

Bethy Pruett died a fair stretch before the sheriff arrived. As if she'd never existed. In less than an hour's time the world changed so much it was as if Pruett had lived the past forty-four years in a vacuum. Deputy Zach Canter called from the ranch and tried to warn the old man off, told him to turn back; told the sheriff his team of deputies could handle everything just fine. But of course, Pruett came.

And when he arrived, he was not prepared. All the talking himself into being ready for the worst did no good. Bethy's frail, elderly mother, Honey McIntyre, held the lifeless body in her lap, quietly stroking that magnificent auburn hair—the hair Bethy had tended to every other Thursday at the salon in town. Dark, chocolaty blood dripped off the porch and pooled in the dirt at Honey's bare, arthritic feet.

Pruett couldn't decide whether he wanted to burst apart or cave inward; he wanted to both scream and be forever silent. In the end he was capable only of doing his job. It was his only handhold on sanity. So he directed his deputies, orchestrated the scenario, as any good cop would. He motioned to Deputy Melody Munney:

"Secure the crime scene, Mel."

"Honey," he said to Bethy's mother. "You've got to let her go. Let us take care of her now." Pruett fixed his attention on Honey McIntyre's red, swollen eyes, avoiding the horror just beyond the peripheral.

"Canter," he said to his youngest deputy. "Gather everyone inside the tack room. Get statements. The barn's heated…no sense anyone suffering this damn chill. Baptiste. You send the ambulance home. Get Scoot and his Coroner wagon. Cordon the whole front of the house, kitchen too. Nobody touches anything."

The remaining sunlight gave up its attempt to escape the horizon and the gloaming sky, suffused by clouds the color of an angry bruise, turned brick red. Night descended then, and quickly. Sheriff Pruett's team continued their mercifully robotic tasking.

"Ty got here in a rush," Zach Canter told his boss an hour later, after the interviews. "They were all inside the kitchen, playing cards. They heard a truck come up the road, a big diesel. Vance Dustin, the hired hand, heard the same thing from the bunkhouse. By all accounts, each of them figured it was Ty, and knew for sure when he started shouting. No one can say for sure what he was sayin' exactly, or who he was sayin' it to. You know Ty. He was drunk and mostly incoherent."

Canter hesitated.

"Tell me the rest," Pruett said.

"Bethy got up and walked out on the porch. All the witnesses said they heard just one shot. It had to be a clean one, Boss. No way she suffered."

"Now that's hard to say, ain't it, Deputy?"

"Yessir, I guess it is."

"Ty fired the shot?"

"Dustin was the first outside," Canter said. "But he was so drunk he was seeing double."

"It's okay, Zachary. Go on."

"They all saw Ty drive through the lawn and down the road to the south entrance. Didn't see anyone else."

"Make casts of those tire tracks," Pruett told Red Horse Baptiste, motioning to the deep impressions in the grass at the corner of the side yard.

The sheriff opened the door to the Suburban and climbed in.

"Where you headed, sir?" Baptiste said.

"I know where he went," Pruett said, and drove away south.

The Willow Saloon was a billiards parlor from the late eighteen-hundreds. Sage, Wyoming, sat eight miles northwest of Wind River, a one-horse town made up of the saloon, a post office, and a small country store. A previous owner converted the upstairs of the Willow from bordello to residence in the early nineteen-hundreds.

Pruett put his hand on the hood of Ty's truck. It was the only vehicle in the small dirt lot. The metal had long since cooled, the engine quiet. The sheriff unholstered his revolver. He checked the cylinders and eased up the stairs, peering through the dirty glass of the saloon door, his nerves dancing expectantly.

Ty sat alone, stooped over the Springfield. A weathered Stetson and a half-empty bottle of Wild Turkey sat next to him on the bar. Pruett saw no one else. Owner and barkeep, Roland Pape, was in the wind. Or worse.

Pruett opened the door slowly. He targeted the sweaty, thinning hair on the back of Ty McIntyre's head. The door creaked loudly, but the old cowpoke remained motionless.

"Sheriff," Ty finally said.

"Yep," Pruett answered, his finger steady on the trigger guard. "That rifle loaded, Ty?"

"Wouldn't be much of a rifle if it weren't."

"You know where Roland is, Ty?"

Ty pointed toward the back door.

"Took a powder," he said. "Weren't much jaw in him. Not like usual."

"Ty, I'm taking you in. Just two ways that happens."

"Takin' me in?"

"I've got big questions need answering," Pruett said. Streams of sweat ran down the nape of his neck and into the middle of his back. His stomach bucked and kicked like a wild horse. His mind screamed at him, questioning, wanting to know why he didn't put a bullet in McIntyre's spine. The law seemed insurmountably distant from Pruett. Frail. Unworthy of such moments in a man's life.

"I said I got to arrest you," Pruett hissed.

Ty did not answer him but he slowly raised the bottle and guzzled from it.

Hate swirled inside Pruett, no chimney for escape. He cocked the hammer of his weapon. The loud *CLACK* snapped the tenuous still of the bar. Ty's head rose up. His shoulders tensed.

"Need you to put those hands on the back of your head, Ty. Slow and easy. Like you mean it," Pruett said.

"Or it could end right here," Ty said. "That's what you was thinkin'."

"End comes in a lot of ways," Pruett said. "It doesn't have to go down ugly."

The tension in Ty McIntyre's back and shoulders suddenly gathered itself. His head tilted back and forth, neck joints popping.

Pruett braced himself. He knew Ty had deceptive, bobcat quickness. The sheriff once saw the old cowpoke punch three college-aged drunks in the face; three in a row before any of them figured the situation.

Pruett put his finger on the trigger, exerting just enough pressure to be a fraction from discharge.

"Ain't no use no more," Ty said, and reached for the Springfield.

When the brain gets nervous, time slows down. It's a coping mechanism. Processing cycles. The sheriff's world dropped into quarter speed.

Movement in the shadows near the back of the bar.

Ty's hand curling around his weapon.

The smoothness of the Smith and Wesson's curved trigger.

Sweat running freely.

Ty McIntyre's skull.

Bethy.

The ache in his heart.

The avenger inside, demanding vengeance:

Him or you.

Then, at the moment he needed to react, Pruett froze.

The soldier training did not fail him. The years of law enforcement experience did not fail him. His mettle did not fail him.

It was his will to live that quit on him.

Pruett eased off the trigger.

Let the chips drop where they might.

Ty McIntyre hesitated, as if he'd read the old sheriff's mind—and then he slid his rifle the length of the bar, raised his arms, and placed his hands on the back of his head. Roland Pape shuffled out from behind a table near the stairs to his home.

Pruett exhaled.

Sick. Shamed.

The sheriff used his left hand to put the handcuffs on Ty. He read the man his rights and escorted Ty out to the Suburban, wishing he could wash the stench of cowardice from his own skin.

The funeral and wake proved nearly unbearable. Pruett's mind struggled for oxygen, drowning deep in a murky sadness. He feigned connectedness with the guests, stomached the canned epitaphs, returned the heartfelt handshakes. All the guests knew Bethy in one way or another and most of them Pruett considered friends. But today they were all outsiders. Spectators on the periphery of his devastation.

And there was Sam, his adult child, returned home only because of the death of an estranged mother; Sam, most peripheral of all. Pruett could not help but think of the biblical story of the prodigal son. In the bible's version, the father waited with open arms. The sheriff's own arms had been closed so long he feared they might never be pried apart again.

Pity confounded Pruett, challenged his self-respect. He knew when given purchase, pity anchored itself to a man's heart, soothing him, making promises—keeping him company in the low hours until a man cleaved to it; until he worried more about it leaving than staying.

Mourners oozed pity. The stench of it emanated from them like perspiration, spoiling the air Pruett breathed.

And the old sheriff felt naked; exposed to the elements: a stumblebum amongst the agile; emotional cripple amongst the stalwart. The barber had trimmed Pruett's gray, thinning hair earlier in town and the old sheriff wore loose, wrinkled trousers tucked unevenly into brown Abilene roper boots. He hid behind a felt-brown, *Charlie 1 Horse* hat; held it before him like a talisman: protection against the omnipotence of the mighty torment in his heart.

Pruett stole glances at Sam. His blood. A part of him. Out of his and Bethy's lives since turning eighteen.

The deputies all stood with their sheriff.

Melody Munney.

Zach Canter.

Red Horse Baptiste.

In the end, Pruett waved as the four-wheel drive taillights disappeared back down the mountain; back the way they came.

Sated by sandwich wedges, comforted by cake, and warmed by coal-black coffee, the mourners and the prodigal child receded.

And the pity receded with them.

The steep south flank of the Gros Ventre range sliced up from the distant coniferous canopy, timeless and severe, sharpened by God's whetstone and left to protect the northwest Wyoming territory like a tyrannical king's castle spire. Sheriff James Pruett stared out through the cold, misting rain. Across the expanse. Pruett land. Twenty-two coniferous acres scattered with a dozen sprawling patches of prairie, full of gorgeous wildflowers and on most days a wondrous, heavenly integrity of light.

The land belonged to the Pruetts since before Wyoming gained statehood. It contained a small family cemetery, marked on three and a half sides by a weathered, two-rail fence. Behind the newly refinished log house, the burial ground sat just past two oak trees that grew together as one in the middle, separating again as they prayed, open-armed toward the sky.

Against the land, the cemetery appeared austere; as cemeteries went, it struck one as describable and unassuming. The Pruetts buried three generations there, including his mother, father, and baby brother, lost in childbirth. They also buried several hired hands there—men from the ranching days who had no other family. Some were from a tribe of Nez Perce who came across the Idaho border in the early nineteen-hundreds—Deputy Baptiste's kin.

Pruett stood before the cemetery's newest grave. The calluses on his palms and fingers paled next to the malignant lesions on the surface of his soul. The icy Wyoming rain offered no purgation; shame and guilt secreted from Pruett's pores, dripping soundlessly with the sweat and rain into the black opening beneath him.

So much of a man got wrapped around the axle over a forty-four year marriage. The task of unraveling seemed impossible; it lay before Pruett, terrifying and enigmatic, like an unfinished nightmare. He spat tobacco into the rivulets of rainwater that spread like spider webs at his feet, then stared toward the heavens.

I always said to do your worst. Guess you were listening.

His old man had been a preacher, but Pruett always found faith a tough nut, even as a boy. And it didn't get better. Things happened in a man's life.

Things done in the name of war.

Things left unsaid.

Only death promised relief.

Memento mori—*everyone dies.*

But while they lived, men grew regrets. And some regrets made strong men emotional wanderers. Pruett's regrets bore *teeth.* Guilt, however, was far stronger than regret.

Guilt swallowed a man's faith whole. Left him with nothing but a gaping, loveless, inescapable void.

And the burden of seeing Sam, his once beloved child—seeing his betrayer firsthand after all these years—caused more guilt in his own heart than Pruett anticipated. It cleaved the sheriff like the honed edge of the sword drawn across an unhealed wound.

Light, diffused by the storm, began its retreat. Pruett could no longer see the spattered earthen floor in the shallow hole. He kissed the cold metal urn and bent stiffly, placing Bethy's ash remains in the ground. He picked up a shovelful of muddy earth, but stopped short of dropping it in.

His wife would have demanded a prayer; would have said no body deserved burying in the ground without some words spoken to God on behalf of its soul.

Anger notwithstanding, Pruett did his best to speak to God:

"We've had our disagreements. Neither one of us lives up to the other. I can't apologize for that now. Don't want to. But I loved Bethy with everything I had. And she loved you. Now, since you took her from me, I am asking you to open the gates of heaven wide. You welcome her into your arms, because she's never done anything to hurt another living soul, and she damn well deserves it. Amen."

He stared again at the shovel in his hands.

Tools felt nothing.

They existed only to make trails for men; to build homes for them; to make their lives more productive.

And tools existed to bury them.

Arthritis seared Pruett's joints as he dropped the muddied earth on Bethy. Towering there in the freezing mist—implement in hand, prostrate inside—Pruett lamented the will of God.

"One of these days
I'm gonna run
I'm gonna leave these fields behind
To find what's over the horizon
One of these days
I'm gonna go
When you look at me
you're not gonna see a scarecrow."

Montgomery Gentry,
Scarecrow

Chapter 2

"CATTLE THIEVES beware."

The auditorium barely contained Professor Hanson's booming voice. The students' chatter pursued a hasty diminuendo. Rustling papers stopped rustling; the girl smacking gum in the front row paused.

The only sound left to Hanson was his ego, serenading him.

Hanson was tall and lanky, with so little fat that his features looked as if they'd been chiseled from stone. He was not handsome, exactly—too skinny for that—but he had an intriguing look about him; a look that drew people in, and his perfect blue eyes looked as if they'd been intentionally etched by a divine artist to fit his gauntness and bring it to life.

Still, were he to stand unmoving at night, outlined in shadow, one might believe a scarecrow had come in from the field for a dutiful rest.

"Given the choice between burning alive or being cut down by a truckload of gunfire," he said, "which do you choose?"

The gravity of the question was intentional—it was, after all, the segue to the lecture's core.

"Another question: would any of you...would *I*...have the temerity to write an entire journal while facing imminent execution?"

Years ago, when a younger version of Hanson had commanded the courtrooms, the galleries came to expect rapture. Lecturing to a hundred college students proved more of a challenge. They constituted a collectively fickle will. Prone to boredom, likely to move in one direction as well as another; they were not unlike pieces of driftwood on the shoulders of wide, ever-changing current.

"Nate Champion, a poor cattle rancher—a man who didn't even own the property on which he ran his nominal twenty head of livestock—was murdered in eighteen ninety-two by the hired guns of the Cattlegrower's Association of Johnson County. Anyone care to guess why?"

No takers. The fear he might pluck a name from thin air was palpable. His reputation from the Law College preceded him, and Hanson enjoyed the ambiance of discomfort such possibility instilled.

"Moving on," he said, mercifully. "It was uncomplicated, like the razing of the countryside while civilization moved westward. The Johnson County War was nothing more than a systemic reality taught to us by history: the politically staked, super-rich—in this case, cattle barons—making themselves richer on the backs of the poor, uneducated proletariat. What happened in this part of Wyoming's history is no worldly mystery. It is a microcosm of the way society has always been.

The words hung there like ephemeral wisps of winter breath.

"Nate Champion made a courageous stand. He owned a single handgun, had a few reloads, and one knife. He took out a few of those who intended to steal from him one of the only valuable things he owned—his life. But it was hard to make do against those kinds of odds. We're talking *Butch Cassidy and the Sundance Kid* here. *Bonnie and Clyde*."

He paused.

"Scream versus the babysitter."

A ripple of laughter.

"There was no storybook ending coming. No hero in the midst. The mob started piling Champion's own firewood against the cabin, meaning to burn him down or flush him out. Either way, the mob didn't care because it was the same end result.

Lucky for posterity, Champion had been writing journal entries all along. While the bullets tore the cabin apart—with his friend lying dead in a pool of blood outside the front door—Champion put down his final testament.

Here is what he wrote last, just before he signed the final page, stuffed the book in his shirt pocket, and broke out the back door to a hail of gunfire:

'Boys, I feel pretty lonesome just now. I wish there was someone here with me so we could watch all sides at once....Well, they have just got through shelling the house like hell. I heard them splitting wood. I guess they are going to fire the house tonight. I think I will make a break when night comes, if alive. Shooting again. It's not night yet. The house is all fired. Goodbye, boys, if I never see you again.'"

Professor Hanson let the words hang there. The symphony conductor, holding forth his baton; the notes still resonating.

"Land," he said quietly. "In the end, it wasn't the cattle. You can own a thousand automobiles, but if you don't have the highways to drive them on, they are just so many parts.

And owning livestock isn't like owning cars. Cattle *breed*. You can grow a herd, *but not if there's no land to put them on.*

Free-grazing, cattle rustling, 'don't fence me in'…it's all about the same song.

Woody Guthrie had a great thought:

'This land is your land, this land is my land'.

But not in Johnson County.

Not then, and not now.

The great state of Wyoming, perhaps more than any other, was built on the value of the land, and it is the value of the land that makes her both wonderful and as dangerous as a merciless, murderous posse."

Hanson stood. Surveyed the sea of flesh-colored ovals. He'd infused them with his interpretation of the song. He walked languidly around to stand at the front of the lectern, his posture both reflective and authoritarian.

"How many have heard of the murder in Wind River?"

A surprising number of hands.

"Brother murdering sister, it's not a pleasant thing. But when one pays particular attention to history, and to the current stakes, not entirely unexpected."

A lone student rose in the center of young adults. Hanson recognized her. Wendy Steele, one of his best students. Older than most of these young ones, yet declared pre-Law.

"I thought you were an attorney," Wendy Steele said.

"Retired," said Hanson.

"I can see why," she said, loudly.

"Excuse me. Ms. Steele, isn't it?"

"I believe the legal system presumes a person innocent until determined guilty by a jury of peers," she said flatly. "One would think a defense attorney to be intimate with this basic core of his profession."

"I think you've found the wrong class, madam," Hanson said in his best lawyerly tone. He was reaching deep for his courtroom swagger. Steele's surety and tenacious accusation surprised him; he needed a reacquisition of equilibrium.

"This is *Wyoming History*," Hanson stated. "My law classes gather in a different building altogether."

"As do your principles, apparently," Wendy Steele said.

A snicker from the rear. A few gasps.

Hanson just stood there.

Statuesque.

Incredulous.

Spellbound.

Unsure of whether his mouth was truly agape or whether it was simply the jaw of his ego.

She'd sabotaged his entire concerto. Skewered him in front of his student body. Worse, he felt an embarrassingly cool attraction.

One predator's respect for the other?

There was no time to decide. Wendy Steele picked up her backpack and, deftly as she had attacked, climbed the stairs, two at a time. Up and away—away from the muted, smitten presence of the great J.W. Hanson.

The wind takes few holidays in Laramie, Wyoming. It sweeps over and down from the Medicine Bow forest. Right to left; front to back; top to bottom. More often than not, it's all of them in the same few minutes. One moment it will swirl in place, aimless and punch drunk—as if it's forgotten what it came for. Then it will suddenly blow all its force directly under a person, rendering them near weightless; as if they will relinquish their belief in the physical laws of the earthbound and fly away.

To the environmentalist, wind is the power of the future. To the physicist, it is not an entity at all but, rather, equalization: air rushing from a zone of high pressure to one of lower.

Pressure and time formed much of the earth. The historian learned the same lesson regarding society. Professor J.W. Hanson knew that history proved society a construct of the various pressures of the ages, both sociological and technological:

Race.

Industry.

Religion.

Classes.

For Wyoming it was the pressure between ranchers and free-grazers; the Cavalry and Native Americans; women and the vote.

Most recently, because of the gas boom in many parts of the state, it was between those with mineral rights and those without.

Hanson actually summarized his own theories of the social strife in an interview he did with a reporter from the *Laramie Boomerang*:

"In every county, township, or parcel, regardless of population or relevance, there is high pressure, low pressure, and the force of greed between."

Friday night at the Buckskin, the crowd surged with the explosive release of a week's tension. A few hardscrabble regulars sat at the bar, but the pool tables and other open areas teemed with young men and women in the prime of their lives.

Professor Hanson sat at his usual table in the corner, near the basement stairs. It was the best observation point in the place and the least likely to suffer the hips and elbows of drunks. One sip into a two-finger whiskey, Hanson noticed Wendy Steele. She was looking at him across the room; a partial smile bent her left cheek, belying the hostility of their first brief encounter.

She walked over, dressed in tight Wrangler jeans, a belt with an oversized rodeo buckle, a white cotton sweater, and red boots. She carried a half-empty bottle of beer; her gait was keen and clearly unaffected.

"May I sit down?" she asked, raising her voice to be heard.

The smile was authentic, so Hanson acquiesced, pointed to the empty chair, and sipped at his drink apathetically. He tried to hide his admiration of her sturdy beauty—tomboyish, unbreakable, she carried both rural curves and soft, womanly swells. Her eyes were haunting, charcoal windows that promised you no access to the complications that lay deep within.

Hanson knew several faculty members who ignored the largely unenforceable rule against teacher-student relations. His own abstinence was far less ethical than practical. Adherence to principle was, in the absence of opportunity, simple mathematical surety. Wendy Steele was a young, beautiful woman with a sovereign intelligence—there was no reason for him to fear the possibility of opportunity, though a strange, oblong throe in his gut made him strangely sorry for the fact.

"As you walked from the midst of my class, you must have been thinking, '*That asshole is not from Wyoming*'."

"I've thought it."

"Would it surprise you to know I was born in Buffalo?"

Wendy took a pull on her beer. "No, but you graduated from Penn Law. You spent your best years in New York. You're no more Wyoming than Wall Street."

Hanson's ego bristled. Externally, he forced a grin.

"Touché." Less pithy than he'd intended.

"And yet you came back," she said.

"*This only is denied to God: the power to undo the past,*" Hanson said.

"Agathon," Steele said. "They teach Greek poetry at the state schools, just like in the Ivy League."

Hanson nodded. "May I add that my evening seemed to be shaping up nicely until your impromptu visit?"

"Look, I didn't come to continue the fight. I came over to tell you I'm sorry."

"Apology accepted," Hanson said.

"May I buy your next one?"

"No, thanks," he said. "I think I'm finished for the night."

Wendy placed her hand on his.

"One drink. A peace offering."

Hanson swallowed his whiskey and slid his hand out from under hers. A sting the color of roses climbed Steele's cheek.

"I'll see you in class," he said.

He pushed through the mass of flesh to the loitering coolness of the Wyoming night.

In class, Hanson purposely skipped over the face of Wendy Steele as he lectured. It was two weeks later when she caught him on his way to the Law School office.

"Could we talk?" she said. "Have a coffee maybe?"

"A coffee?"

"We're adults. Coffee seems innocent."

"I don't think so."

"I *did* apologize. And I wasn't hitting on you."

"Imagine my deflation."

"I don't know what I was trying to accomplish before. Seems I can't get the words right with you."

"Maybe," Hanson said, sitting down on a short stone ledge, "there just isn't much to say between us."

"You don't believe that."

"Maybe not. But that doesn't mean it's not true."

"Dinner tonight," Wendy said. "Your place. I'm inviting myself over."

Hanson smiled. "I don't cook. Epitome of the savage bachelor."

"Pizza, then. Use your bachelor skills to dial up a pie. I'll bring cold beer."

"Grinders," Hanson said.

"What?"

"The Buckskin does these delicious meatball grinders. I'll call down and you can pick them and the beer up before you come upstairs to the apartment."

"You live on top of the *bar*?"

"Eight o'clock."

"Nice space," Wendy said as she flopped down in Hanson's reading chair. "Not as noisy as you'd think. Being above the bar, I mean."

"We're actually in the back. Over the storeroom. It works."

Hanson felt uncomfortable in his own skin. Or apartment.

Wendy pointed to the wall, inside a nook where a piece of framed art hung in a remodeled space built for a flat-panel television.

"Great painting."

Hanson put four of the six Railyard Ales into the fridge. "One of the only extravagances I allow myself."

"That's a Chardin?" Wendy said, kicking off her boots.

"*Glass of Water and Coffee Pot.*" He opened the beers and joined her, sitting across from her on the matching leather loveseat. "What exactly are we doing here, Ms. Steele? I don't generally hang out with students."

"I've never cared for you much," she said.

"Not exactly fit for print, is it?" Hanson said, taking a long swallow from the sweating bottle. "Not newsworthy, I mean. You more than made that point in the classroom."

"I've always been impressed by you, though. That is, of course, a different thing."

"Consider me commensurately flattered. But impression is no reason to approach a man and invite yourself to his bedroom loft."

"Is *that* what this is?" she said.

Hanson could not categorize her tone. It bothered him. He'd made a career reading people—facial expressions; nervous ticks; eye movements—*tone* was elementary. Prelude to the *coup de maître*. With this one he was stumbling amidst the planted fields of his own repertoire.

"Your last test score was abysmal," Hanson said.

"Test score?"

A basic tripwire. Diversion.

Jurisprudence for Dummies.

"Your grade. Down to a C. Even in a state school, that's not a good sign."

"I, uh…right. I mean, I know."

Hanson stood, walked to the kitchen.

"Grinder?"

"Yes."

He brought the food back on paper plates, along with two more beers; the aroma of sweet marinara tantalized his hunger. When he sat this time, he leaned slightly forward, intentionally stealing a bit of the space between them. She was a strong woman, but still, unschooled.

"Why are you here, Ms. Steele?"

He felt better. Control was back within his grip, gelatinous and unwieldy as it was. He took a large bite of the sloppy sandwich—it was *delicious*.

Wendy did not answer him. She nibbled at the crust of the baguette.

"I am related to the McIntyres," she said finally. "Ty is my uncle. So what you said in class, you were speaking of my family."

"I had no idea. I can see why I offended you, and I apologize."

"Maybe. I mean, no. You were just talking about it in the way anyone would. But the way it affected me, the way it stung me. Well, it caught me off-guard. I've never been close to them. To any of my family, really. My father and I haven't spoken in years, and uncle Ty…well, like my father, we were nothing alike. I let my emotions get the better of the situation."

"We're all vulnerable to a moment."

Wendy Steele looked away, back to the painting.

Hanson stood and retrieved the last two Railyard Ales.

"He went against the style of his era," Wendy said.

"Sorry?"

"Chardin. When most of the others were painting grand masterpieces of ornate, asymmetrical complexity, Chardin did his best to capture the simple, beautiful truth at the core of existence."

"*One makes use of colors, but one paints with emotions,*" Hanson said, quoting the painter.

Wendy turned from the painting. Tears brimmed on the edges of her exquisite bottomless eyes. A singular drop crossed the barrier of her control, running a true line down her flushed cheekbone and into the darkness of shadow below.

"Family is the damndest thing," she said.

"That it is," Hanson said. "My father died when I was in my thirties, already deep into my law practice."

"I'm sorry."

Hanson waved her off politely.

"He was a good man. Moral. Just a baker, actually, but his turpitude is what caused me to take up law. I saw how honest and unyielding he was. Law-abiding, I remember always thinking. Then he got sick. Stomach cancer. Really one of the worst ways to go. Painful.

So my father, this man of principle and morals, he lies. Lies about the severity of the pain early on so that he can hoard enough opiates under his mattress so that, when the pain becomes very real, he has more than enough to end it."

"Oh my God," Wendy said.

"He didn't want it to look like an overdose. That's why he hoarded the pills. He planned the whole thing out. Just increased his dosage each day. Pill by pill he put himself to sleep."

Wendy crossed the small space between them and knelt, putting her arms around him. Hanson's eyes, though, were dry; his voice was steady.

"It's not that I blamed him. He did what he had to do. No one suspected. It was me who found his stash—the pills he still had stockpiled. I never told anyone, not until now."

"He must have been in tremendous pain."

"No, he planned for that too. The doses he was taking would have assuaged his suffering. He was a smart man. He knew what he would need to kill the pain and he knew what he would need to kill himself. It was then I decided to devote my talents to defending the accused. You see, I realized at that moment that any man or woman can be driven to something they would ordinarily never consider. Those people need someone on their side."

Her face moved close in, eyes locked momentarily with him. Lips moved together, his mouth opened in surprise, hers with confident passion.

She kissed him. She tasted of beer and smelled of vanilla cream. She reminded him of all things in the world he believed to be sensual. Hanson was a little drunk. He pulled her close. Unable to deny himself. They stayed like that, entwined, exploring each other with hands and tongues. They stood as one and moved to the bed.

The last sex Hanson had was three years prior, with one of the mousy librarians from the Special Collections branch at Coe Library. Liza Dexter, he remembered suddenly. It had been perfunctory lovemaking and had done nothing to assuage his fears of having gotten too old to be any good in bed.

With Wendy, Hanson rediscovered his youth. Because they'd been drinking, they were less restrained; they wrestled passionately, discovering each other's' shapes, needs, and desires. He was easily twenty years her elder. Probably more like thirty. Yet she cleaved to him as if he were the only man in the world. She made him feel not only younger but relevant. As if he'd not spent the better years of his life alone.

They made love for over an hour. Fell asleep in each other's arms. The heat of her lithe body infused him with hope.

In the morning, Hanson did not want to move. He woke first. Wendy lay there, delicate as a bird, still pressed unobtrusively against him. He was relieved. The last thing he wanted was for her to awake and realize her horrible misjudgment—relegate him to the purgatory of bad drunken choices.

She did awake. And as soon as she did, she squeezed him harder. Kissed him deeply. They made love again. Slower. More intimate than the night before. Hanson allowed his newfound confidence to guide him. Still she intimidated him, and he strove to show her that he was worthy.

I've never cared for you much.

There are times when hearing what you already know to be true is the most unbearable accusation of all. Even as situations change, such words remain lodged in the back of the heart like splinters. They fester. Infect the better times with accusatory concerns.

Was it possible?

Did Wendy Steele come to his bed in order to garner his services? Could her motives be so tactical?

"Back to your uncle Ty," Hanson said, breaking a palpable yet comfortable silence. "You came here to ask me if I would defend him."

Wendy avoided his eyes, measuring her response. She kissed his cheek.

"I think so. I've never really been one to use subterfuge. The whole idea of asking it now feels pretty unseemly."

"I suppose it's only subterfuge when you've not been candid regarding your motives," he said.

"My motives aren't as clear as they once were."

"Just like that?"

"Maybe. Or maybe I am just rethinking the whole 'get involved' option. Me, I mean. With my family. Not with you."

"In matters of family," Hanson said, "we're always involved. Whether to engage. *That*, my lady, is the dilemma."

Wendy nodded solemnly. Her dark eyes conveyed caution. And what else?

A defeated admiration?

"What would you say if I *did* ask?"

Sitting there, mesmerized by the reawakening this young woman had produced in him—deserted to an extent by his own conscience and principles—Hanson wasn't sure there was anything he would not be willing to give her. He stroked her cheek and kissed her on the top of her head.

"I'd say no."

"And those people in Black Mountain
are mean as they can be.
Now they uses gun powder
just to sweeten up their tea."

Janis Joplin,
Black Mountain

Chapter 3

PRUETT STOOD outside Ty McIntyre's jail cell with a plate of hot food from Casa de Zenda. Proprietor Zenda Martinez served the food and took care of the books. Her husband, Roberto, set the authentic Mexican menu and cooked the food.

Ty lay on his back, knees up, boots flat on the mattress.

"Lunch," said Pruett.

Ty looked over with his eyes only.

"Brung in from where?"

Pruett opened the slat in the door and set down the tray of steaming refried beans, crispy flour quesadillas, and sweet rice.

"From next door."

"Pruett," Ty said and got up from his bed. He walked to the bars, leaned against them. He extended a thick, callused hand.

Sheriff Pruett stared for a moment, finally accepting Ty's meaty, sandpaper paw. It was just something you did.

"Ain't much in this world I'm sorry for," Ty said, "but this is one time. I loved her too, though I never said so."

Pruett felt the barbaric strength in McIntyre's grip. A nervous flutter ran across his backside. He'd let his guard down. Miscalculated. The gun was holstered on his right side. If anything went down, he'd never be able to cross-reach for it with his left hand. Not in time.

Ty smiled, as if he knew the chess game going on inside the sheriff's brain. His lips peeled back in a hangman's smile, exposing battered, wood-colored teeth. He released Pruett's hand, picked up the tray of food, took it back to his bunk, and started eating hungrily.

The sheriff walked the hallway back to the office. He again felt cowardly. It was not a feeling he planned on befriending. Maybe it *was* too soon to be back. Baptiste and Munney argued against his returning so soon, and only with what candor they could muster. It was clear that he was pushing the line, but that was how he lived and worked; he wasn't planning on changing that. And Pruett prided himself in his ability to detach from the personal. He knew how to work; how to put the job first and be a sheriff.

But after the stupid mistake back in lockdown, he now wondered if he'd misjudged the place of his heart in all of it. No one would blame him, but that wasn't the point. He would not be able to stand the look of his own mug in the mirror.

Back in his chair, shame and fury swirled in his head like a chimney fire. Fueled by the self-embarrassment of his failure back at the Willow Saloon, he returned to Ty's cell.

"I'd kill you if duty didn't say otherwise," Pruett said.

Ty did not look up from his plate.

"Guess I have it coming," he said.

"You do," Pruett said. "But my *job* is to treat you like any other. Let the jury decide and the State hang you."

"Don't hang 'em in Wyoming anymore, Sheriff. You know that. It's been a few years at least."

"You and I never cared much for one another, Ty. But I'm guessin' we both loved Bethy."

"I always thought highly of you, Sheriff. Really I did, no matter what me or some of the fellas mighta said on a drunk occasion or two. You're a good man, sir, and over the years, I became grateful you found Bethy and did right by her. You always treated me fair, too, every damn time I was in the poke."

Ty was a brawler and a drunk and had spent many nights cooling off in the very cell that he now occupied. "Is that all you come back to say?" Ty said.

"No," said Pruett.

Ty looked up at him with coal-colored, scurrilous eyes.

"Then say it."

"I don't know what happened on the ranch for sure," the sheriff said. "I know what you already said. Your pa and brother aren't saying anything else. Neither is Honey. I would advise you to get a lawyer and follow suit."

"Already happenin'," said Ty. "Niece in Laramie is tryin' to gather one up. Some professor."

"A professor?"

"Like that'll help, I says to her. But she said to shut my trap just the same."

"Give a shout when the food's done," Pruett said. "I'll send a deputy."

"I meant what I said about sorry," Ty said, returning to his plate. "But just so we're clear...I won't be sayin' it again."

"I meant it, too," Pruett said. "All of it."

As the sheriff walked away, a cold line of sweat ran down his spine. The gun on his right hip felt dense; as heavy as the world atop his shoulders.

McIntyre boys stacked hard time. Life in many ranch households left few choices for the sons—or sometimes even the daughters. Fathers wore the ranching mentality into a boy, long and relentless. A rancher's son would unlikely ever choose any other type of life. Psychologists called such conditioning institutionalization. Ranchers passed it forward decade by decade, century by century. Not a rite of passage but rather an inheritance of duty, burned hotly and deeply into a child; as permanent as any brand.

Ranch country made for a hard living. The land was unkind to those who worked it, so families sometimes became commensurately unkind to their own. Few, however, were as unkind to their own as the McIntyres.

Ty's father, Rory, inherited the entirety of the McIntyre property when his own father died of a weak heart. Two-thousand upper acres of rough terrain and hayfields; a lower four-thousand acre parcel. The ranch house, a barn, a stable, two corrals, and all the heavy equipment were on the lower piece. Rory's two brothers had died early in life; young, in their twenties. Rory's father found the pair, trapped and frozen in a surprise fall blizzard while moving the last of the cattle down from the upper McIntyre place.

Rory married and Honey gave him four sons in a row before he drew a daughter. Ty was the youngest of the boys and a year older than Bethy. Still, he was the best ranch hand, as well as the toughest and the meanest. Ty easily wrestled calves for branding when he was eight and could buck a bale of hay faster than some adult men could when he was ten or eleven.

When he was thirteen, a man named Sketch Borland made a wisecrack about Ty's cereal bowl haircut. The boy lit into Borland like a small bobcat tearing into a grizzly ten times its size. Borland was no fighter, and a bit of a drunkard, but he had at least a hundred pounds on the young boy. The rest of the crew had to pull little Ty off the older man.

Ty's brothers—Rance, Cort, and Dirk—were tough too, in that order and according to age. But Ty could handle them all. One at a time or together.

Like Ty, Rance and Cort had parcels of the ranch. The two of them rode saddle bronc and bareback almost every summer weekend at the rodeo grounds in Wind River. Dirk did not ranch. He worked as a crack rider for an outfitting business that caravanned tourists and hunters in and out of the Wind River Mountains.

Ty considered them all pussies. Dirk because he rode soft horses for a living and never did rodeo. The other two because Ty had never really considered it rodeo to ride any animal less angry or dangerous than a bull.

Bulls bloodied and broke Ty into pieces throughout his life. Doctors pinned together and replaced parts of him so many times that against the gloaming light you could see his spine make two distinct turns, like an S-curve on a mountain road. His face had been stomped so magnificently one Friday night that his head swelled to double its size, his face grape-colored and horrifying. It healed mostly, but stayed as cratered and uneven as the surface of the moon.

Over the years, hardship took several inches off Ty's stature, but those same years added twenty pounds of mass, too. A thin layer of wintering fat hid fresh, sinewy muscle, and more than a few pounds of angst.

Ty McIntyre was getting old, but he was still a man most would rather see on the other side of the street.

Returning to Rory McIntyre's ranch was something Pruett had been putting off. There were many reasons. He wanted to think that the fear of seeing the spot where his wife died wasn't one of them, but the old sheriff knew better.

As Pruett stepped down from the truck, Rory opened the screen on the front door and stepped out, a cup of coffee in his left hand.

"James," Rory said.

"Rory. How're you holdin' up?"

"Life don't allow for men to spend much time mournin'. Work needs to git done."

"One way to look at it," the sheriff said.

"Ain't no two ways about it. You comin' in or can we do this while I git the wagon rigged up to the tractor?"

"Wagon is fine," Pruett said.

He followed the old bowlegged cowboy toward the barn where Rory started throwing spools of baling wire and boxes of staples onto the hay wagon.

"Shoulda offered you a coffee," Rory said. "Honey's in the house. I can yell for her."

"I'm good. Not planning to stay here long."

"Looks like you wintered okay," Rory said, gesturing to the sheriff's stomach.

"I did all right."

"I was rememberin' all the times you and your family came out here for brandins."

"Never missed one that I can recall," said Pruett.

"You got knocked on your ass more than a few times," Rory said.

"Sure did."

"You liked my little Bethy, even back then. Always lookin' after her more 'n yourself."

"Been fond of her long as I've lived and breathed, I reckon," Pruett said.

"You've always knowed my mind on the subject."

"I know you never liked me," the sheriff said.

"Liked you just fine. Thought you were lazy, is all."

"Someone put cow shit in your cereal bowl this morning, Rory?"

"Just conversation."

Pruett tried to understand. Believe it wasn't personal. Most ranchers he knew didn't have much respect for any other way of life. They might tolerate you, even befriend you—but it was a closed society.

"My family's been working the land as long as any McIntyre," the sheriff said.

"Not ranchin', though. You wouldn't claim that."

"Not by your definitions, no."

"Dirt farmers," Rory said.

"You got a hornet you want to put under my bonnet this morning," said Pruett. "I'll tell you now, old man: you don't quit on the idea, you're gonna find your huckleberry."

"Fair enough," Rory said.

He'd never once looked Pruett directly in the eyes.

"I did all right by your daughter," Pruett told him. "Best leave it at that."

"Not sayin' you didn't. Not tryin' to cling to the past, neither. Doesn't mean I won't jaw on it from time to time."

"Bethy was wearing your coat and hat when she was killed," Pruett said.

"Yep. So?"

"Well, she brought her own coat, didn't she?"

"Mine was closer."

"And you were all playing cards."

"Euchre."

"What?"

"We was playin' euchre."

"So you're saying she grabbed your coat because it was closer to the door?"

"Yep."

"And hat."

"Say again," Rory said.

"Your hat. She was wearing your hat, too."

"If you say so."

"I'm just trying to make sense of all this," Pruett said.

"Are you? I'm glad for that," Rory said, and opened a can of chew. "Dip?"

"Trying to cut back," said Pruett.

"What for?"

"Doc's got me on a regimen."

"Doc Percy?"

"Is there any other?"

"Percy's a quack. I wouldn't let him doctor one of my animals."

"My other question, Rory, is why Bethy was getting up anyway?"

"Huh?"

"It's your house. Ty comes roaring up the road with piss in his veins—I'm just wondering why you didn't go out to greet him."

"Why *I* didn't?"

"Yeah, why *you didn't.*"

Rory seemed to be letting that one settle a bit. He removed his sweat-stained hat, rubbed a patch of gray whiskers, and spat on the ground.

"Hmm. I guess she just jumped to it first."

"And put on your coat and hat."

"And put on my coat and hat. Christ, Pruett, is this the best you got to be doin' right about now?"

"Just procedural, Rory."

"Fuck procedure, Pruett. That's my daughter you're jawin' about."

"Just trying to get all the facts straight."

"Well I got fences to mend. We done here?"

"Just about," Pruett said. "You aware that Ty's saying he doesn't remember anything?"

Rory nodded. "Blacked out as usual, I guess."

"Might have some more questions for you and Honey a bit further down the road," Sheriff Pruett said.

"We done?"

"We're done, Rory."

"Goddamn right we're done," Rory mumbled as the old codger threw a tool belt over his shoulder and mounted the tractor.

Pruett sat on the wide rocker swing on his front porch. His boots rested comfortably atop the flat pine rail, toes pointed toward the expanse of the Wyoming night sky. The cloudless night opened up unabashedly before him; a foreboding conduit to the heavens. The umbrella of stars glowed exquisitely; pinpoints of diamond light floating atop innumerable fathoms of insatiable blackness.

Pruett's index finger stirred the glass of clouded whiskey. The aroma drifted upward. Pungent and sweet. Inviting and unsettling. His stomach circled and snarled within him like a cornered animal.

He'd purchased the bottle of whiskey almost a month before at the Wooden Boot—the bar had a package liquor store with a drive-up window. Pruett purchased it with a resolve that he *would not* crack the seal, hoping the gesture alone would both assuage the ache in his soul and calm the demons.

But it seemed over the weeks all the disjointedness and fear and lonesomeness leaked down and gathered in one tepid pool in his chest, solidifying there like a huge, rounded stone.

Pruett looked up into the vastness of the universe. All week he'd dreamed of a drink. He told himself it was because he was willing to do *anything* to counter the overarching pain in his soul. But that wasn't true. Not entirely.

He had put the bottle away. Taken it out again. Played the old game of angel and devil on the shoulder; good cop, bad cop. Teasing himself. Knowing that in the end it always came down to himself; who he was at his core.

And how fervently he needed to numb the pain.

Twelve years of sobriety was not something Pruett took lightly. He'd been through several sponsors. Unlike most tenderfoots, he worked a job he loved. And there was the truckload of determination that it took to stay sober every single damn day of that dozen years. Drunks didn't count by years; they counted by minutes. They clawed their way until enough minutes made an hour and then enough hours made a day.

Pruett had no idea how many moments there were in twelve years, but he'd thought about having a drink in damn near every one of them.

But so far, he'd withstood.

Then, that morning, going through the box of mementos Bethy stashed behind the dresses in her closet, Pruett discovered a single sheet of parchment paper. A weathered eight by ten cardboard folder frame.

A birth certificate.

Samantha Wendy Pruett.

The prodigal daughter who dropped Samantha and now answered only to "Wendy".

The sheriff drained the orange booze in a single, fluid motion. He poured himself another. Then a third. This time he paused. The feral warmth of the whiskey washed down over the immovable stone, loosening it some; it also tamed the restless animal in his belly.

Losing his wife was a terrible thing, but there were memories that cost him nearly as much—and proved just as impossible to outrun.

Pruett heard the car before he saw the headlights. He did not get up as Wendy Steele walked the path toward the house. The two hadn't spoken more than a dozen words in the past few years, including at Bethy's funeral. There was a time when Pruett wanted nothing more than to forgive her, and to ask the same in return. He figured after Bethy died, seeing his child would reignite those desires.

It did not.

She'd married Todd Steele, a local ranch boy, straight out of high school. Mostly, the sheriff always thought, to spite her old man. The two annulled the marriage less than a year later. She kept the Steele surname and joined the Peace Corps. Anything, it seemed to Pruett, to stay away from Wind River. Away from him.

"Can I come up?" Wendy said from the bottom step.

"Give it a try."

She climbed the steps slowly, walked over to the table, and stood next to the extra chair. It had been her mother's. Pruett motioned for her to sit.

"You look underfed," Pruett said.

"Thanks."

"More glasses inside," Pruett said, waving an arm toward the front door.

Wendy shook her head slowly. "I'm okay. I thought you gave up on that stuff."

Pruett did not answer. Wendy sat down.

The two withstood the silence for a while, soaking in the peace of the Wyoming night. Pruett finally dropped his boots to the solid decking. A gesture. Prelude to saying what had been wandering around in his head all day.

"You know, you're allowed to hate me all you want, but you didn't have to let it keep you from visiting your mother. She never did anything but love you, girl."

"I always hated it when you called me that."

"Hmmm."

"A punctuation mark on the inevitability of chance. A son would have been nice."

"I never regretted a thing about you. Except your leaving."

"I didn't drive up here to talk about this. I came to talk about uncle Ty."

Pruett drew back. "Your *murderous* uncle Ty, you mean."

"Maybe. I figure a jury will decide that. But he's still family. He's still Mom's brother, and she loved him."

"She did love him," Pruett said, "and he'*ll* sit before a jury of his peers."

"I guess it surprises me to hear you say that."

"How's that?"

"I don't know. You never struck me as the merciful type. Now with what happened to Mom, well, I just..."

"You seem a little matter-of-fact about the whole thing yourself. Did you think I would have already strung Ty up in his cell?"

"No. I didn't mean it that way. Honestly, Sheriff, it's because I would understand. However you are feeling."

"Speaking of hating a name. When exactly did you start? Referring to me in the professional, I mean, rather than the paternal."

"You never did understand. I always meant it respectfully."

Pruett poured another drink for himself. "You know, I had my reasons. I never asked for that medal. It would have been wrong to accept it."

"Because you didn't deserve it."

"That's right, because I didn't fucking deserve it," the Sheriff said.

"Makes people wonder why," Wendy said.

"See, that's the difference between you and me. Always has been. Man who murdered your own mother deserves more mercy than..."

"Than?"

"Than your own father."

"I didn't drive up here to open old wounds."

"You've said that. Why *did* you drive up here, then?"

"You know, you *hated* your old man. Why should it be any different between us?"

"Maybe it shouldn't," Pruett said. "But you owed *her* a hell of a lot more."

"I did owe her more. And honestly, I owed you more too. That's the real reason I drove up here."

"That and to tell me you got an attorney for your uncle Ty?" Pruett said, sipping on his whiskey.

"That too. Though he hasn't said yes."

Pruett did not answer for a long moment. When he spoke, he measured his words:

"Ty carved out his life, just like the rest of us. People put themselves into their own drama. There's due process; setting aside personal feelings and doing what the job says you do."

"You feel like that's in the cards—Uncle Ty getting a fair shake?"

"'Course I do. It never ceases to surprise me, the way you see your old man."

"Yeah, well, I asked you to defend yourself a long time ago. So did a lot of people. You declined."

"A man shouldn't have to defend himself to those that love him."

"Sometimes that's all he can do."

They sat quiet for a bit, again awash in the peace of silence.

"The booze isn't going to help anything, you know."

"Not a thing I care to debate with you," Pruett said. "You're a long way from knowing what makes things better or worse for me."

"I'm with him. The lawyer." Wendy said. "I didn't plan it. It's reckless. But it's the kind of thing that chooses a person, rather than the other way around."

"What's his name?"

"Jay Hanson."

"Congratulations," Pruett said, and finished another glass.

Wendy didn't respond and Pruett didn't get up when she left.

The whiskey no longer held back the coldness of night.

In nineteen-ninety-eight, the Army decided to award the Soldiers Medal to a pilot and three crewmembers that landed as part of a helicopter evacuation and ended up putting themselves between their own U.S. comrades and fleeing Vietnamese villagers in the Hamlets of My Lai.

The team, led by Warrant Officer Hugh Thompson, Jr., stopped American troops from further firing on unarmed civilians. Specialist Four Jimmy Pruett was a door gunner, and one of the team who were to receive the decoration—the highest award the Army gives for bravery not involved with direct enemy conflict.

James Pruett made history by choosing to become the only United States veteran ever to turn down the Army's prestigious award. The story made national headlines, in large part because Pruett refused to communicate—publically or in private—his reasons for refusing to accept the honor. The act generated significant speculation that his refusal might represent a silent protest against a false tale of heroism; that perhaps the military was once again trying to spit shine an otherwise horrendous event by drumming up a handful of convenient heroes.

Pruett knew that wasn't the case. It took a hard will to keep his reasons to himself. He knew that Thompson and the rest of his team acted just as bravely as suggested—more so, actually. Pruett could not guess how many innocent lives the men saved that day. Yet the only images in Jimmy Pruett's mind—images that still burrowed their way into the nightmares of Sheriff James Pruett—were the ghosts of those innocents brutalized and murdered *before* they arrived; slaughtered by soldiers representing Pruett's own country—his own chain of command.

For Pruett, the decision was simple: he could accept no award— no honor—for an event so heinous, carried out by his fellow compatriots. He never begrudged or dishonored those who accepted the medals. He loved them like brothers, though he knew his refusal forever cast a shadow across the glint of their heroism. But he also knew that, ultimately, orders begat action—and orders came from on high.

To James Pruett, there could be no honor salvaged from such a day.

The press, they'd wanted answers. And when they didn't get them, they assumed there was a cover-up. They did not understand. No one did.

It also took the town of Wind River a long time to reconcile the reasoning behind Pruett's silence. In truth, Pruett figured they never really did comprehend it better than anyone else did; the townspeople simply accepted him back into the community. Like a mother opens the door for a wayward son. Reasons become less important than the faith of family.

The deepest wedge driven, however, was between Pruett and his daughter.

"An innocent bystander
Somehow I got stuck
Between a rock
and a hard place
And I'm down on my luck"

Warren Zevon,
Lawyers, Guns and Money

Chapter 4

THE HONORABLE Bridger C. Butler descended from western royalty and he intended that the network news crews know it. There were at least a half dozen national news organizations sent to Wind River, Wyoming, to cover the "Land Murder" case. Butler called a public briefing only an hour after learning of his selection; judges from Rock Springs served on a monthly judicial rotation to travel north one hundred miles to Wind River and it was Butler's turn—through the randomness of arbitrary schedule pooling, Bridger Butler would adjudicate the trial of the decade; a true, Western, cowboy murder.

"My great grandmother was defeated only twice in a sharpshooting match, both times—narrowly, I will add—by none other than Annie Oakley," Butler told the press. "A good-hearted, philanthropic woman by all accounts, my granny. She started a family that has now lived in this great state for three generations. That I have been given the opportunity to preside over a case that touches so close to the historical nerve of Wyoming is a privilege to me, an honor to my family, and will become a testament to my adoration for this great state."

J.W. Hanson shrugged at the judge's prepared remarks. No doubt Butler *did* love Wyoming. But murder cases like this one sprung up very rarely in such small western communities. And such trials made careers.

The national attention would make Hanson's job both easier and much more difficult. He knew how to play big trials. It was a problem of media management—give them too little information and you lost a chance to play on public sentiment; give them too much and you might as well hang the client yourself. He'd also done his research on Butler: the man appeared to be a fair magistrate, concerned most with the meticulous application of law. Butler supported the death penalty but tended toward a more liberal view of the rights of the accused. Hanson also knew peripherally of his tendency to ride prosecuting attorneys. Butler made no secret that he saw the prosecution—with its myriad resources—as a bully in the making.

All other things being equal, Judge Butler tended to subscribe to the idea of "innocent until proven guilty". That would help the defense, but the McIntyre case promised to be an uphill struggle. Ty had motive to want to kill his father and brother. Not much financial gain in the killing, but revenge? Yes. And Ty was violent. His arrest record alone supported that. Never mind that every member of the jury would know it.

If he were to accept this case (as if he had not already agreed the first night he made love to Wendy Steele), Hanson needed a strategy. How to lay out his case for this defendant. Hanson smiled inwardly.

There was *always* a strategy.

Hanson needed to be alone. He drove westward out of Wind River, toward Jackson Hole, cruising along highway 191 until he reached Hoback Junction, where instead of going on to Jackson he veered left on highway 89 toward Star Valley. He'd taken the route before once with his family, traveling to Idaho Falls for some school shopping decades past. He remembered the road shadowed the great Snake River as it twisted and turned through a vast canyon leading eventually to the Wyoming-Idaho border.

The views did not disappoint him. Steep granite walls rose up on one side of the road, signs every few miles warning of falling rock— indeed Hanson saw chunks of the mountain resting scant few feet from the narrow shoulder of the road that would have crushed a car such as his. Twice he had to swerve to avoid smaller pieces of rock— smaller, but still a foot or two in circumference; enough to tear off a wheel or snap his axle and send him caroming into the raging Snake River to his left.

Such moments aside, the picturesque drive was exactly what the lawyer needed. He'd fallen so fast and so hard for Wendy that he was simply incapable of cogent thought in her presence. It bothered him. He did not like the lack of control he felt when with her, particularly since he was certain he already wanted to spend the rest of his life with her.

He knew such feelings were likely akin to infatuation and perhaps not strong bedrock on which to build the foundation for the rest of his days, but he didn't care. His life was over half past him and he'd spent too much of it conforming to standards, laws, ethics, methodologies, ideologies, and lesson plans. It was time to accept a bite from the apple, as egregious an act as it might represent. He longed for the lure of a life lived past the boundaries of conformity.

In Wendy he had certainly found that. But the case—the forthcoming trial—that was no playground for him to rediscover opportunities lost along the way. Ty McIntyre's life hung in the balance, not to mention justice for Wendy and Sheriff Pruett.

Hell, he thought. *The entire town deserves some kind of resolution.*

But those truths were part of what gave him trepidation. Yes, there was indeed the conflict of Wendy's relation to the defendant— Hanson was still weighing the implications and possibilities inherent therein—but decades spent thundering in courtrooms taught him that rarely did such cases deliver a balancing of Lady Justice's scales.

Too often families and communities walked from the hallowed courtroom jaws agape at the travesty of the legal system, stunned to be leaving with far more questions than answers.

Hanson wasn't sure he could bear returning to the brutal fight, at least not then, when it would mean—win or lose—the inevitable tearing of family bonds and the excruciating, palpable rile as the true law—the law Hanson and every other seasoned attorney knew intimately, with its weaknesses and insufficiencies and outright unfairness—spun through the courtroom like a twister, napalming innocent, law-abiding people with the ferocity of its inadequacy, crushing optimism wherever it was found, and, worst of all, jading the hearts of those who believed in it the most.

But who else, then? This was the itch he could not scratch. The trial was going forward whether Hanson stayed and fought on behalf of Wendy's uncle or he tucked his tail and retreated in cowardice to the comfort of his benign faculty existence. Wendy, Sheriff Pruett, Ty, and the rest of the community were going to be dragged through the glory of the legal process he so many years ago denounced, whether he stood with them or not.

So he would stand. Of course he would.

And as he had so many times before, even after countless months on end roiling in the belly of the broken system, he would believe once more.

Believe that he could make a difference.

The jury selection process began two weeks later.

Voir Dire: "to give a true verdict", or in the case of jury selection, *to tell the truth.*

Hanson was wary of the prosecutor in the case, Town Attorney Beulah Jorgensen, having done due research on his opponent. Jorgensen was a congenitally dislikable woman the professor had not met himself but about whom there seemed no shortage of stories or public opinion. The unmarried woman spent much of her childhood henpecked by the girls of Wind River and ignored or ridiculed by most of the boys. Her position as Town Attorney afforded her, it seemed, the chance to readjust the balance of the scales. Despite (or, perhaps, because of) her demeanor, Jorgensen had a near-perfect record. The woman had not lost a case in well over a decade.

Jorgensen was also seeking the death penalty. A charge of first-degree murder was the only crime in Wyoming punishable by death, and there had not been an execution in the state in over thirty years. Aggravating circumstances were a requirement. Hanson read the relevant portion of the charges levied by the State of Wyoming:

"In planning the shooting, Ty McIntyre, the defendant, did show the premeditative forethought commensurate with first-degree murder and in shooting toward a house with multiple occupants, any of which (or any combination of which) would be put at risk of imminent death by his own hand, did knowingly create a grave risk for the victim of the crime as well as additional persons."

Voir dire was less about getting at the truth and more about a study of human reactions: expressions, tone and timbre of voice, directional glances—the indicators were myriad and since the balance of the case was about the jury, expertise in reading people was requisite to choosing twelve men and women that would deliver the desired verdict.

And the *last* thing the accused wanted was a jury of his peers. Hanson learned just a few trials into his defense career that true peers were less likely to sympathize, more apt to convict. He taught it this way:

"Look at your coworkers. They may like you, but there is always that underlying sense of competition, of 'who's getting the next promotion?' Peers tend to have *too much* affiliation. They are biased and don't even know it."

Why should he get away with murder?

Why should she get rich quick?

The thought between the lines was always the same:

Instead of ME?

A good defense lawyer wanted a person who, though obviously *not* from the same background or race or employment, could put themselves in the shoes of the other. The perfect juror had what Hanson referred to as "transferrable sympathy"; the tendency to have pity on those whose lives seemed worse off than their own. And it was *that* propensity he sought. No peer conflict, just the innate ability to *imagine* themselves in the other's predicament. Hanson, and all good trial lawyers, knew that imagination offered jurors wide latitude in thinking about what a person might do under such circumstances. Too often, a jury of peers was likely to deliver a guilty verdict—it was too much like self-judgment. That is why prosecutors loved jurors who looked, talked, acted, worked, and played just like the accused. Twelve perfect peers would convict every time.

Hanson liked to use an approach where he created a scenario, tried to put the entire prospective panel in a moment; one they could *feel.* Then he would ask them to imagine the answer to a particular question—many times one that contradicted the constructed scenario.

For example, he might ask them to close their eyes, place their minds in a nursery: two walnut cribs, walls painted neutral green, identical twins—boys; strawberry blonde hair, only a few months old. Perhaps there was a mobile hanging from the ceiling, a littering of stuffed animals, a changing table with diapers, ointments, and wipes stacked on the shelves. Then Hanson would ask the jurors to imagine large swaths of blood marking the walls; the babies, not breathing, death all around and the parents accused.

He'd watch the individual reactions. Horror, surprise, shock, anger. And almost always, there were those who appeared less jolted; not exactly unaffected, but willing to see the process through to the end. In these instances, the prosecutors often succumbed to the moment, as shocked by his "antics" as much as many in the jury pool. But in such reactions, Hanson learned what he needed to know, while his adversaries missed the crucial cues. The selection process was akin to a speed match of chess. One could not afford to miss the smallest potential disadvantage or the tiniest breach in the front line of the opponent.

Another favorite technique involved Hanson regularly eliminating jurors without a single question or conversation from or with either attorney. He would call on a juror only to thank them for their service and excuse them. The strategy was again fairly simple—it required Hanson only to dismiss a juror outright, one who already mismatched his profile. The reaction of the other jurors, however, could be telling.

"Juror seven. Ms. Cornwall?" Hanson asked, though he knew her name.

"Yes, sir," Dorothy Cornwall answered.

Hanson noted fear in her voice. "Thank you very much for your time today, dear," he said to her, then addressed Judge Butler: "Your Honor, the defense would like to use a preemptory challenge for juror seven."

The judge nodded. "Ms. Cornwall, the court thanks you. You are excused, ma'am. Will the rest of you please move forward one chair, including those of you in the alternate chairs and the gallery. Thank you."

When the reshuffling was complete, Hanson addressed the juror who had just been moved into the box. "Juror number thirteen," he said. "Ms. Bineford? I hope I got that right."

"You got it fine," Suzan Bineford said.

"Could you see yourself as a vigilante? What I mean is, under a particular circumstance, might you take the law into your own hands?"

"I don't think so," Bineford said. "Not to such an extreme, no."

Hanson expected her answer and followed with: "Ever have any cause to scrap with any of your brothers or sisters?"

"'Course I have," she said, agitated. "Who hasn't?"

Hanson liked her. He didn't want to press further, wary of a Jorgensen challenge. He'd gotten her to decry vigilante justice, hoping that might sway the prosecution favorably.

The juror selection continued for most of the day. By four-thirty, the attorneys were ready to agree on a jury. Five men, seven women, and two alternates. Hanson excluded as many male ranchers as he could, but of the seven men on the jury, five of them ran cattle in rural Wind River. One was a teacher—a professed conservative with what Hanson believed to be some pretty strong liberal underpinnings he probably dared not flaunt before the local school board. The five women posed a challenge, too. They'd either sympathize with Bethy McIntyre or believe Ty when he talked about how much he loved his sister. They'd mother him or hang him; it was Hanson's job to steer them.

On the way out of the courthouse, Beulah Jorgensen stopped him. "Mr. Hanson," she said.

"I told you, Beulah. Call me J.W."

"I don't care for people who use initials to refer to themselves," she said. "And I don't recall asking you to use the familiar with me."

"Understood," Hanson said.

"I thought it only fair to tell you that I am planning on calling your, uh, well, friend, to the stand. Ms. Steele."

Hanson feigned stoicism. "For?"

"To testify as to the violent potential of Ty McIntyre. They have a history," Jorgensen said.

"She won't say anything to impugn her uncle, you know," Hanson said.

"She'll say whatever is the truth or I will have her jailed, sir."

"You do whatever you have to, ma'am," he said.

"She'll be on my witness list," Jorgensen said and exited into the fading light.

The short conversation with Beulah Jorgensen squatted on his brain like a toad. Hanson sat on the edge of the hotel bed, a cable news channel humming in the background. He tried to call Wendy when he returned from the courthouse, but she either was out of range or was not answering. At around eight o'clock, she slipped through the door.

"Where have you been?" Hanson asked.

"I had dinner with a high school friend. I told you twice yesterday, and once today. When you were getting ready to leave for court."

"Right," Hanson said. Jorgensen's revelation that there was a history between Ty and Wendy that played well for the prosecution perplexed him. He was also annoyed that neither his client, nor his girlfriend, had found it relevant to share said history with the lawyer tasked with saving the man's life.

"A curmudgeonly little bird told me today that there is a 'history' between you and your uncle Ty," Hanson said.

"Of course we have history," Wendy said. "He's my *uncle*."

"I neglected to expand. I believe one might call it a *violent* history."

Wendy sat heavily on the bed, next to Hanson. "Oh," she said.

"I appreciate the candor, though I'd hoped for a less-incriminating response. Seeing that I will be trying to keep your uncle from a lethal injection starting Monday."

"It was a long ways back. I didn't think it would matter," Wendy said.

"Jorgensen is calling you as a witness for the prosecution. To show Ty's propensity toward violence."

Wendy closed her eyes and lay down on her back. "When I was sixteen, my dad and I started to disagree a lot. We had some pretty bad arguments. Uncle Ty broke one up, that's all that happened."

"Wendy, if that was all that happened, Beulah Jorgensen would not be planning to call you to the stand."

"Ty took a swing at my dad. He missed. Gave me one hell of a shiner."

"Shit," Hanson said. "Charges?"

"It was mandatory because I was a minor. But the sheriff testified that it was an accident. My dad said that he and Ty were fighting."

"Which wasn't the whole truth," Hanson said.

"It was *enough* of the truth," Wendy said.

"Had Ty been drinking?"

"Ty was always drinking. So was my father."

"What happened in court?"

"The attorney defending Ty asked for a trial by judge. Figured the sheriff testifying would hold more sway on another member of the justice machine. He was right. The judge threw the case out."

"And Beulah Jorgensen?"

"She was just starting out in the City Attorney's office. It was one of her first cases, I think."

"Perfect," Hanson said.

"Sorry," Wendy said. "I really didn't think it mattered, since he was acquitted. Pretty stupid."

"Hopefully it won't matter much. She can't go after you too hard. One, you were the victim in the previous case. A child to boot. Second, no conviction. Guessing we won't have the sheriff's kind remembrance of the events in question, though."

"Pruett wouldn't lie," she said.

"He's not my biggest fan."

"What reason is that?" she said.

"Come on, Wendy. I'm closer to *his* age than yours."

"Pruett has his problems," Wendy said. "But he looks out for my happiness."

"He pulled me over when I first got into town. Did you know that?"

J.W. Hanson had been leaving the Wooden Boot after one draft beer and a few questions directed at the bartender and a couple of the regulars. Halfway to his hotel, blue and red lights appeared in his rear view mirror. He pulled over and a man who looked like a walking oak tree got out of the patrol car, donned a proper western hat, and walked toward the professor's Toyota Prius.

"License, registration, proof of insurance, sir," the big man said, leaning down, and a bit into the window.

"No problem, officer," Hanson said, handing over the documents.

"I work for the Sheriff's department, Mr. Hanson," Pruett said, looking at the license and other papers. "Not an officer of anything I know of."

"Sorry about that," Hanson said.

"Your insurance card has lapsed, Mr. Hanson. Last week."

"Guess I forgot to put the new card in my wallet. You can call my agent—I'm still covered, I assure you."

"I don't doubt it," Pruett said. He directed the beam of his flashlight into Hanson's eyes. "Wind River's a nice place, Professor. It stays that way because the rules get followed."

He handed the license and laminated card back. "Big trial coming up. Hope for Ty McIntyre's sake you don't let *his* insurance lapse."

"Message received, Sheriff."

"No message, Professor. Just get your new card."

"You should have told me," Wendy said. "Pulling you over is a load of bullshit."

"Easy, lady. Nothing happened. He was just pissing across the bow of my boat."

"It still doesn't mean he won't tell the truth," she said.

"The evidence suggests your uncle Ty killed your mother—the man's wife. I'm not expecting any flattering testimony from a witness like that. I'd be a fool."

"Tonight it's a bottom,
tomorrow, what then?
Anything that brings a happy glow
Once I loved somebody,
I wish I could again
How far down can I go?"

Lefty Frizzell,
How Far Down Can I Go

Chapter 5

BOOZE HAD him by the balls. Pruett knew it. His conscience told him to ignore the negative; that circumstances allowed him to make significant concessions. But there wasn't much denying the reality that the bitch was back. Pruett only too gladly let her right through the front door, though the one thing he'd forgotten was that her grip rivaled any vise he ever owned.

Reaching rock bottom requires a devastating personal journey, no matter the person; bottom being as far down as a man or woman can go. Alcohol does not smooth the stones, illuminate the path, or sooth the senses—at least not for long. Rather, it catalyzes the horrors, accelerates the downward journey—like pulling the trapdoor on the gallows. One is enticed into believing alcohol dulls the nerves when it ultimately only intensifies the pain.

Pruett gave up drinking years before—twelve years, two months, and a handful of days. Back then the reason was simple; clearer than anything had been for a long, long time: he stopped because his wife asked him to stop.

Should he have stopped before?

Did his health ultimately depend upon his stopping?

Was his career, his family—his *honor* at stake?

Yes to all.

But being aware and being capable were two different things. One of the many challenges of the addict is the paralyzing terror resiliency faces when eclipsed by the towering shadow of *NEED*.

Pruett felt it every morning when he climbed stiffly out of bed; that clawing desire for the next drink. He heard it from around every bend, flying on the very wind: the whispery promise of release.

Whenever he was drinking, the bottle held full sway over Pruett; a flagon of demons that manipulated his thoughts, the beasts scrambling constantly to gain further purchase on the craggy slopes of conscience and morality.

But after thirty-two years together, after Pruett's awful betrayal, Bethy sat him down, looked him in the eye, and *required* something of him. All the other years, from the first to the last—every decision that impacted their lives: each belonged to him. But this one thing—

this one impossible thing—she wanted. And so it was actually not that hard for him to do.

After such a long hiatus, one might think it hard to return to such a low point, but the sleazy lie of a drink fixing what ailed him returned too easily. It seeped into every crack and fissure in his soul, feeling like a smoky-keg fire, soothing the aching joints of his heart. Soon enough, he knew, the warm liquid salve would cool, freeze, and expand, bursting the façade of his healing into a billion dead, sparkling pieces.

The demons returned too, happily resuming their elevated position above his will. Like snipers in the trees bordering his mind, they aimed their weapons, demanding that he do things that, until then, only came to him in nightmares; evil thoughts that now breached the innocent light of day.

Blue smoke choked the air in the small bar. Pruett liked to drink in the Wooden Boot—one of three Wind River bars—because of the clientele: mostly roughnecks from the gas patch, many of them transplants. The locals that frequented there were a rough bunch too, and kept mainly to themselves. Ty McIntyre hung his hat there some nights, when he was a free man anyway. Tourists avoided the Boot; it was dingy, seedy, and could be downright dangerous. Because of these untoward realities, however, it was a popular hideaway for people who shirked the public eye.

Sheriff Pruett was off-duty and wearing a plaid hunting shirt, jeans, and a fresh pair of Justin work boots. His felt hat occupied the stool beside him on the right and he had just drained a third Heaven Hill blended whiskey when Carter Lee Holcomb walked up and dropped his butt in the stool to his left.

"Sheriff Pruett," Holcomb said, tilting back his natty, sweat-ringed straw hat but leaving it fixed atop his head. He motioned to the bartender. "Jenny. Two bourbons and a Bud back."

Holcombs were about as popular in Wind River as McIntyres. Sonny Holcomb, the father, ran one of the two local filling stations; twenty-year-old Carter Lee worked at Jonah Field for a Canadian natural gas company, *Encana*, doing miscellaneous scuttle work—

roughnecking, mostly. That is, when he wasn't drinking or roaring his truck up and down Main Street, cruising for high school seniors or drunken divorcees.

Pruett kept quiet and tilted his head back to Jen Werner, signaling for another Heaven Hill.

"What, you don't talk to us respectable folk anymore?" Carter Lee said.

"Would you mind adding a little clarification, slick?" Pruett responded. Though it was a rough bar, he never pushed his sheriff weight around unless it was necessary. Most of the regulars respected the distance between him and the badge. In a place like this, even the law could remain anonymous.

But to Carter Lee Holcomb, no one got a free pass. Carter Lee was every town's fallen high school hero. Three years before he'd made Wyoming All-State in football. Halfway through his senior year, with no real college prospects, Carter Lee dropped out of school and started working the gas fields. He put on fifty pounds that first year, most of it padding the considerable muscle on his short, wide-body frame. Word in town was that Carter Lee's biggest contribution to the old man's business was drinking away what little profit Son Holcomb's station mustered.

"Fuck you, *boy*," Carter Lee said, his eyes looking at Pruett in the mirrored backstop. "Heard you keepin' old Ty *fuckstick* McIntyre all nice and fatted up in the jailhouse. Probably sneaking him his favorite whiskey too. Just saying that maybe you ought to think about the good respectable folks in this town 'stead of catering to the scum."

"First class, eh, Carter Lee?" Pruett said. "That what I have sittin' next to me? Well, shit, I am honestly sorry. Here I was thinking since you walked in here that the God-awful stench of white trash came right in here with you."

Pruett normally controlled himself better than this. He never allowed himself to be bullied into a bar fight; you couldn't carry out the office he held and have an unchecked temper. But the sheriff had been drinking. And "fed up" didn't begin to describe the assault he'd been feeling against his awful, inflammable pride.

"Least I don't lower myself to playin' grab-ass with my own wife's *killer*," Carter Lee said.

James Pruett didn't *jump*, so much as *explode*, sideways. When he drove his shoulder into Carter Lee Holcomb, he hit the man so hard it lifted Holcomb clear of the barstool. Pruett kept moving, as if he was carrying a practice dummy across the field, doing a fine football crossover step as he barreled through the five or six empty barstools between them and the pinewood wall at the front of the Wooden Boot.

As Pruett carried the stunned man through the air, Holcomb's arms and legs flailed wildly, like a windmill that had lost its equilibrium. When Pruett slammed Carter Lee's back into the solid wall, the man's lung spewed a final reserve of breath, his red face went pallid, and the fight drained from his eyes. Pruett let Carter Lee drop mercifully to the floor, both the oxygen and the mighty pith stolen from him in just a few short moments.

The big man leaned down, face to face with the young roughneck—who was still searching for his wind—and looked him straight in the eyes: "You be careful who you think to bring up in conversation, Carter Lee. Next time, there won't be any stopping it."

The fight awoke a different kind of demon inside Sheriff James Pruett. Once the fever of bloodlust took him over, he felt rejuvenated—reborn—as if he could *physically* challenge his pain; as if he could bust his guilt the way a crack rider broke a wild mare. It felt so *good* to put Carter Lee Holcomb down.

Later, on his front porch, nursing his bum knee, he realized he'd not felt this good since long before Bethy died. There was a time in Vietnam when a young, scared boy decided it was time to find himself or get sent home in a bag. Some kids never figured that out—or at least they never were able to summon the requisite courage.

Pruett took a pull from a bottle of Beam and remembered the jungle hooch his platoon discovered one rainy afternoon, marching through the tangled middle of the Quang Tri Province. The sky still bellowed heavy rain, but the sun was also out, and water was literally turning to steam the moment it landed on the heated branches, leaves, and soil. It gave the whole scene a mystic, otherworldly feel.

And so a sense of deep foreboding came over PFC Jimmy Pruett when his commander instructed him to clear the small villa; a feeling of dread so overpowering that he froze for the first time in his forty-two days in country. Jimmy Pruett stopped in his tracks halfway to the entrance to the hut; fellow soldier PFC Jo-Jo Barney, walking half a step behind, nearly ran him over. The platoon commander barked at Pruett to move ahead, follow his orders.

But Pruett couldn't move. He thought of his girl back home; he remembered the ashen, blood-caked faces of the friends he'd already seen zippered and shipped to a first-class burial in the States.

Eventually the platoon commander pulled him back by the straps on his pack and sent another man in his place. The hooch was empty, abandoned for weeks. That evening, when the platoon dug in and set up a perimeter, no one spoke to him. But they whispered to each other. Nineteen year-old Jimmy Pruett knew what was on the men's mind: the putrid danger of a coward in their midst.

You could abide almost anything in the bush. You came to admire—and even *love*—all sorts of people you probably wouldn't stand within ten feet of back home. The most popular guy in the platoon—Rag Top Willy—was a good old boy from Texarkana who admitted one night to Pruett that he'd once viciously beaten a black boy for nothing other than the color of his skin.

Yet some of Rag Top's best friends in the platoon were black, and though they knew his story, these self-respecting men trusted Rag Top—and Rag Top trusted them. Men would abide almost anyone squatting in the hole next to them if it meant they'd likely wake up for another day—because waking up for one more day meant you were that much closer to going home.

But a coward?

Cowardice had its own color. If you abided a coward, you might as well be carrying a one hundred eighty-pound grenade with the pin pulled; death was just a matter of time.

PFC Pruett stewed all day. He pretended not to notice the sideways looks. He'd been a popular soldier right from the start, but that was fading fast. He volunteered for point on that night's patrol. The fact that the countryside all around them was hot as a fry-cook's griddle only made PFC Jimmy Pruett happier: he prayed all day to find Charlie out there in the jungle; knew the only way he was going to redeem himself was to choke down that motherfucking fear and get some.

Kill or be killed. Either way, Jimmy Pruett was returning to camp a goddamned hero.

The patrol found the shit, all right—came upon a small contingent of Vietcong who were unaware how deeply the Americans had penetrated into their perimeter. The eight members of the night patrol killed all nine of the Vietcong encampment without firing a shot. PFC Jimmy Pruett killed two for himself. He also took a finger from every enemy killed. When he returned to the camp, he stood in the middle of them—those who'd returned with him, those who were trying in vain to sleep, those who stood post. Eventually the platoon gathered around him. PFC Jimmy Pruett—the soldier who failed them earlier; the man whose courage had become an ever increasing doubt in the minds of those he'd sworn to stand beside and protect—laid the gook fingers down, one by one, in a small pile that resembled kindling that might start a small campfire. Jimmy Pruett shined his standard issue flashlight on the trophies for exactly one minute. He timed it on his watch. Sixty seconds of silence; one minute of a prayer-like atmosphere. Then he extinguished the light and crawled into his sack.

He fell asleep without ever saying a word and no one questioned the courage or the will of the soldier named Pruett again.

"I focus on the pain
the only thing that's real...
...the old familiar sting
try to kill it all away
but I remember everything"

Johnny Cash,
Performing
Nine Inch Nails,
Hurt

Chapter 6

THE BADGE of the Sublette County Sheriff's Department was really a simple thing, made of something like thirty percent silver and the rest Pruett didn't know what. He was no metallurgist. It was a five-point star with the word "SHERIFF" arced across its top and another five-point star with some basic stenciling that had an Old West feel to it. There were only six things Pruett demanded his deputies to know about the symbol they wore over their hearts:

The five points represented their mission as officers of the law.

Peace.

Service.

Loyalty.

Protection.

Honor.

The sixth was that he expected every one of them to be willing to lay down their life for any citizen of the County of Sublette, which they served. It wasn't in the oath, but James Pruett made them swear it to him.

Pruett polished the metal with a callused thumb pressed beneath a shirttail. He put the badge down on the table and reached for the bottle. He half-filled his glass tumbler and drank until it was empty. The smoky whiskey reached his bowels and stoked him like a furnace.

Words.

Fucking words.

Ideology.

The drunker he got, the more he felt like a fool for building his principles on ideas so vaporous. Great words felt invincible in the strong man's heart but when confronted by the hardness and unfairness of life became as weak as rice paper cast into the fire of Hell.

The sheriff's plan was not impenetrable, but it was solid. Two possible outcomes and either assured that Ty McIntyre paid his debt. The planning came natural to Pruett. The will to act, however, came only from the booze. The oath James Pruett swore when he took office was very real to him; a resonance of the honor in which Pruett's old man so strongly believed. He spent the past four decades dedicating his life to the honor of upholding laws that stood against the very kinds of selfish acts occupying his mind since his wife's murder.

Two men struggled to control Pruett—one, the honorable sheriff; a man dedicated to law and to justice. The other man—the *devil* inside him—claimed that justice was not only blind, she was a deaf mute, shackled by an overworked court and trussed so thoroughly in red tape she would likely never come close to completing her tasks.

Pruett's hardened heart—the heart hardened by anger and a vengeful hatred of the perpetual loneliness under which he now woke and ate and worked—wallowed in the muddy slop of hatred and revenge. The sheriff was not young. He'd long ago accepted the reality that every man owes a death. No one knew the where, when, or in what fashion. But one could *choose*. One could decide whether a death meant something to the living; whether or not it cleared a column in the balance sheet. Pruett did not fear dying. Death introduced itself to him in the villages and hamlets of Vietnam—exposed its true nature; the nature of the cowardly jackal, waiting patiently to steal scraps from the lion—from *life*, the *true* predator.

Pruett learned that it was *life* that was incapable of mercy; a beast that brought forth not an ending, as would death, but rather a continuance of anguish. Life drew out his pain, the grand horror show in his mind, eyes permanently seared open to watch. Now with Bethy gone and the devil in his veins, Pruett decided that rectifying his mistakes meant doing something his conscience and his creed decried.

Nothing in the world worth owning comes to a person without a price, he reminded himself when his conscience made its protestations. And James Pruett knew the price of peace. He'd seen much more selfish acts; acts that bore no ends and whose entire nature lived in their means.

Pruett intended to reach an end; an end, he hoped, to the pain. And somewhere deep, in a place he could ignore for only so long, he realized what he needed the moment he saw Bethy curled in a pool of her own lifeblood. The *means*—the creation of the perfect opportunity—took some figuring.

It was a Saturday when Sheriff James Pruett made an intentional oversight in the assignment of Sunday patrol. Wind River bars did not open on Sundays, so the department's rotating schedule had only one cruiser on duty throughout that day and night. The deputy scheduled to handle the second of two twelve-hour patrol shifts that Sunday, Melody Munney, received a call from the sheriff Saturday afternoon:

"Hey, Mel, how's the weekend so far?" Pruett asked. He reached her on her cell, at the lake.

"Not bad, Sheriff," Munney said. "Something wrong?"

"No, no. I need to know if you can switch shifts with Zach. Give him your Sunday night shift, take his on Monday."

"No sweat. Just means I get a full day of skiing in."

"Thanks, Mel."

Pruett knew Deputy Munney would stay at the lake; her parents owned a cabin there and Melody and her friends spent every off-shift day up there in the summer, particularly on the weekends. He never made a second call to Zach Canter, who told the sheriff he and his wife planned to spend all day Sunday in Jackson Hole—riding the tram, catching a movie, and then dinner at *Nani's Cucina Italiana*. Deputy Canter would not be home until late Sunday night.

Sheriff Pruett now had the whole day to himself with the prisoner. The riskiest part of the plan was the second step. Pruett intended to drive Ty's pickup from impound to the parking lot at Eagle Heart trailhead four miles into the Bridger Wilderness, and then to jog back down to the jail. If a witness spotted the truck, the sheriff risked identification.

The weekend prior Pruett tested the effects of Valerian, an herb with natural sedative properties and, more importantly, not part of basic toxicology screening protocol. He gave himself double the recommended dose for his body weight. The effect took about twenty minutes to kick in, and though it didn't knock him down very quickly, he did sleep soundly for five hours in the middle of the day. For Ty, Pruett added a little past double, giving it to the prisoner in his Sunday night dinner—a dinner the sheriff picked up and delivered late, around nine o'clock P.M.

"Damn, sheriff. My insides were startin' to touch," Ty said as he plowed into the plate of fried chicken and skin-on mashed potatoes from the Wrangler Cafe. He drank the tainted milk in several gulps.

"Leave the plate by the door," Pruett said.

Outside in the main office, the sheriff changed his department coat for a jean jacket and his own hat for Ty's dove-colored *Stetson*. He jimmied the key locker with a screwdriver from his desk, scarring the wood. The keys to Ty's impounded truck hung on the far right peg, where Baptiste put them a month before. He checked his watch. The Valerian dose would be kicking in soon. The plan gave Pruett a little over an hour and a half to deliver the truck to the Eagle Heart Park trailhead and trek the four miles back to town.

The sheriff didn't see a single car in town. He drove Ty's truck on the back roads, keeping clear of Main Street, until he reached the turn to Skyline Drive. Skyline was the only road up above the lake to Eagle Heart. He passed one or two tourist vehicles coming down the other way from the lake, but no locals. He parked the truck in the lot at Eagle Heart and then jogged back down to Wind River, taking to the shadows of the barrow ditch whenever a vehicle approached.

Ty lay on his back, snoring loudly, his right arm splayed into space. The dishes sat on the floor next to the cot, food half-eaten. Pruett unlocked the jail door and picked up the tray. He turned to face the cell entrance and held the tray as if he were carrying it away, then walked quickly and slammed his forehead into the steel frame. The blow caused an explosion of light in his head as Pruett launched the tray and its contents into the corridor. The empty milk glass shattered against the far wall as Pruett fell to the ground. The collision of skull on steel hurt more than he planned. Blood ran from a gash on his forehead, coloring both his uniform and the tile floor. As coherence returned, he pushed the blood around some on the floor: the smears of a struggle.

Ty's inert body was heavy, corded muscle hidden beneath the orange County jumpsuit. Pruett wrapped a kerchief around his own forehead and slung Ty over his shoulder in a firefighter's carry. He kept most of the blood off the unconscious man's clothing but made sure he left behind full fingerprints from the escapee: on the keys, the screwdriver, and on each door leading out of the jail, into the office, and down the back stairs to where the sheriff's Suburban waited.

This time leaving the office, Sheriff Pruett turned on the overhead red and blues. He drove fast, as a sheriff would after an escaped prisoner, spewing gravel as he fishtailed out of the parking lot and leaving black marks where he took to Main Street.

The moon cast a day glow on the forest. The air was crisp, the winds silent. Ty McIntyre woke slowly, clacking his dry mouth, thick with thirst and head as heavy as a bowling ball, Pruett guessed.

"Where the fuck..." Ty said, trying to get up on an elbow.

As he became more aware of his surroundings, Pruett knew, he'd stop struggling against the effects of the tranquilizer in his system. Ty McIntyre was smarter than he came off. He lay in the dirt, no doubt waiting for his senses to come back to him. He moaned a little.

"Shut up," Pruett said. "Don't let your mind give you too much courage, Ty. I'm armed, and I can see you just fine down there, mulling it all over."

Ty remained on the ground. The slur in his speech real. "Shhuriff. Pruett. Fuck's goin' *on?*"

"Ain't Sheriff tonight," Pruett said, pining hard for a shot of anything. He'd known he couldn't afford for them to find alcohol in his system, whichever way this went. The twelve-hour lack of booze welled up inside him like a dry-heaving geyser and he put a boot into Ty's ribs.

"AHHH, shit," Ty shouted, curling into a fetal ball and grabbing his side.

"Came here to break a promise," said James Pruett. "Sometimes a man's got to, Ty, if he's going to make things right."

"The fuck happen to yer skull," Ty asked, looking up, squinting at the dried blood around Pruett's wound.

"You attacked me when I was taking your food out."

"Hell if I did," said McIntyre.

"Oh, you did, Ty. Sure as you murdered my Bethy, you shoved me into the cell wall, stole the keys, and drove your sorry ass up here to beat trail into the wilderness."

"Fuck that. Never stick, Sheriff. You had to drive my carcass up here. Cain't explain that, I imagine."

"Nope. Not unless your truck got here before me."

Ty looked up, the puzzlement on his face evident in the moonlight.

Pruett continued. "Down in the parking lot. Seems after you worked me over, you broke into the locker and got your keys. The rest ain't hard at all to figure."

"You call the others?" Ty said.

"Funny thing," Pruett said, standing now, gun pointed at Ty McIntyre's head for the second time in as many months. "Radio in my Suburban got itself sabotaged. Seems you thought of everything before you broke yourself free."

"Might as well get the thing over with," Ty said.

"Need you on your feet," Pruett said. "Can't have any bullet trajectory theories chasin' after me. Caught you on the run, as you probably guessed. I don't suppose you'd mind getting to your feet. I'll give you a little head start and…"

Ty rolled quick, three times, barreling into Pruett's shins and toppling him so hard it reopened the cut on the big man's forehead. Pruett hit the hard forest ground with a loud thud of dust and a pinecone struck him in the kidney. His hand was suddenly empty, pistol flying through space into the perimeter of night.

The old cowpoke kept bull rushing him, digging his boots into the ground, never giving Pruett the opportunity of space to get his bearings or an advantage. Soon the sheriff was flat on his back, Ty on top of him with iron legs holding Pruett's ribs like he was a bronco. Then Ty's fists went into a terrible windmill of punches, most connecting with the body as the sheriff turned his head away and down. One of Pruett's arms was pinned, but when Ty slowed the barrage, the other reached for a thick branch and brought it straight into the side of Ty McIntyre's head.

The force of the blow would have finished the fight in most men, but Ty McIntyre was a tough-as-turpentine, bull-riding cowboy. The branch did move his position off balance a little, though—Pruett could feel it—so the sheriff rolled *with* Ty's body instead of against it. The sheriff felt the balance of power shift in his favor. He put his arm around Ty's neck and tried to get him in a chokehold—Pruett's only chance now against the younger, tougher opponent, but before he could lock up, Ty grabbed him by the shirt lapels, and used the force of gravity on the downhill portion of the forest floor to go into a backward somersault.

Pruett saw his world flip over and suddenly his opponent had those vise-like legs wrapped around his shoulders and neck. Ty then began squeezing the life out of Pruett. The sheriff struggled, swinging haymakers impotently through the cold night air, but as the velvety blackness washed in around the borders of his vision, Pruett stopped.

Kill or be killed.

Of the two outcomes, this one was the more honorable.

"It's dark and it's dreary
I ponder in vain
I'm weakened, I'm weary
My repentance is plain."

Bob Dylan,
Beyond the Horizon

R.S. GUTHRIE

Chapter 7

SHERIFF PRUETT awoke, not knowing where he was or quite remembering how he came to be lying on his side. Pain assaulted him from several angles, mostly bunched into his spine and twisting like a funnel cloud. He did not move right away—he was not sure he could or should. And as he lay there, the sharp cold of the night chewed through his uniform and jumpstarted his senses.

Disorientation drained from him slowly, replaced by a sick realization:

Ty had not killed him. The prisoner was now a fugitive—one with God knew how many hours head start. With a little luck, the trail of evidence Pruett left behind on McIntyre's behalf might just keep the sheriff out of jail.

As Pruett tried to roll from his side on to his stomach, the pain seared him, racing up his back, spreading like tendrils through sinew and bone. When he finally got to his stomach, he did a pushup and tried to get his boots under him, but he only got one before the dizziness put him back down.

"Might want to stay down a bit," Ty said, cracking the silence. He took a drag on a cigarette and blew the smoke into the black forest. "Hope you don't mind, I snatched these from your truck up yonder."

"Shit," the sheriff said. "How long I been out?"

"An hour," Ty said. "Maybe two."

"You didn't run?"

"No place to run from it, Sheriff. 'Sides, I've had time to think—time with a thousand square miles of empty wilderness starin' me in the face. Fightin' you, that was all instinct. I ain't never done nothin' *but* fight people and things my whole life. Other kids. Honey, my ma. Bulls. Don't matter; they all had me fight 'em at one time or another.

Not now. Not after what I done. This time I'm paying the piper outright. No more debts owed to the house."

The two sat in silence for a while.

"I'd have killed you," Pruett said. "If I was able, I mean."

"I should've let you," Ty said. Then a mean laugh leaked from his lungs. "Jesus, Pruett, you couldn't ever have handled me. Not in your best days."

Pruett said nothing. Everything hurt—his conscience most of all.

"Didn't know you smoked," Ty said.

"I don't," Pruett said. "Melody, she can't keep 'em in her squad car, 'case her boyfriend catches her in town for surprise lunches. She hides 'em in my Suburban so she can sneak back to the courthouse every few hours."

"Sounds like the lady has trust issues," Ty said.

"We all have trust issues."

"How we going to work this out, Sheriff?"

Pruett thought about it. Funny thing, the anger that consumed him before was gone. He felt stupid. Bethy would have hated what he'd done this night. "I guess that's up to you, Ty."

"Yeah, suppose so. Guessin' if my lawyer got a bite of this he'd turn it into a pretty good mouthful."

"Yep," the sheriff said.

"Wouldn't look too proper for you, though."

"What I did was wrong. I'll take my lumps," Pruett said.

"Nah," Ty said, standing up and offering the sheriff a hand. "It's done. I told you, I ain't runnin' from this. Pretty much gave up that notion when I decided to stop off at the Willow Saloon. Knew you'd catch me there, Pruett."

Back at the parking lot, Ty lit another.

"Guess I better drive my truck back down. We can play it all out the way you had it. 'Cept you caught me 'stead a killin' me, that is."

Pruett stood quietly in the darkness. "You could run, Ty. You know this wilderness as well as anyone around here, except for maybe Dirk."

"Not runnin'," Ty said.

"Well, if you are staying, I'll see to it there aren't any additional escape charges filed," Pruett said.

"That'll work."

"We'll leave your truck here. I can have Canter and Baptiste pick it up tomorrow. Be kind of hard to explain how it was I let you drive it back down."

They climbed aboard the Suburban. Pruett didn't use the handcuffs. On the way down, Ty spoke.

"I told you I wouldn't say 'sorry' again, but that don't mean I can stop feelin' it, Pruett. Sis, she was the only person ever saw much good in me. Pretty sure she was wrong, but damn if it didn't feel good to know you had someone like that in your corner."

"She was a decent woman," Pruett said. It still hurt him to refer to her in the past tense.

"We off the record?" Ty said.

"We left the record a few miles back, I'd say," Pruett said.

"I meant to kill 'em all that night," Ty said. "Ma. Rance. Cort. It's just what a man's supposed to do when persons of low character try to rob him of his birthright.

That's McIntyre land. All of it. Weren't to be played like a goddamned hand of *poker*. Luck of the draw? Nossir. Got to be more honor in it than that. Ma shoulda knowed that much."

"Pa, you mean."

"Yep, pa…what'd I say?"

"So this about those gas rights, then?" the sheriff said.

"About more than that, Sheriff. It's about family. Don't have to love each other, just gotta believe in one for all. That kind of thing."

"You try reasoning with them? Sober, I mean," Pruett said.

"Oh, hell yes. Wouldn't hear a word of it. My fucking old man. He's worse'n me, tell you that right now. And my brothers? Better part a Rance and Cort ran down my momma's leg."

Pruett nodded in the blackness.

"You kill anyone in the war, Pruett?"

The sheriff thought about his answer. "Yeah, I killed some."

"It more right, you shooting some poor Charlie a hundred thousand miles away in some God-forsaken jungle? More right'n me shooting someone who's *blood*, considerin' they stole my family inheritance?"

"It was the wrong blood that got spilled, Ty."

"Goddamn it, Pruett, I never meant to harm a hair on little Bethy's head."

"I believe you," the sheriff said. "I know you never meant to hurt her. Look, your issue isn't with me anymore, Ty. What you did is murder in the first. The law doesn't care what you intended, or your reasons for doing it. It doesn't matter that I killed some gooks halfway around the world and it doesn't matter you didn't mean for it to be Bethy."

"Don't matter," said Ty. "I'm tellin' my lawyer to plead me guilty in the morning."

After putting Ty back in his cell, Pruett tried to clean himself up. He decided not to call anyone in. Were the situation to have played out as the evidence suggested, Pruett would have handled it alone anyway. He wiped up the blood and tried to disguise the extent of his injuries. Make it look like Ty got the worst of it. Jorgensen would want to tack on the assault and attempted escape charges, so Pruett needed to make sure he kept the drama to a minimum.

He didn't feel tough anymore, nor was there courage seething in his veins. He felt foolish, and it wasn't a feeling cared for.

Revenge. It's a word most have thought about at least once in their lives. But when Sheriff James Pruett swore his oath he was supposed to have risen above things like revenge and drama and savageness; he was supposed to uphold justice and honor and dignity—and most of all he was supposed to follow due process.

He'd done none of those things since Bethy was shot and killed. Oh he didn't always fail on the external, like tonight, taking a prisoner north into the wilderness to murder him for what he was *alleged* to have done to the sheriff's wife. Many of his failures were on the inside where no one could see them.

Pruett knew that's how most people lived, though few would admit it.

He pulled the bottle of whiskey from the lower desk drawer—an old bottle of Rebel Yell he'd gotten as a gift for one holiday or another, before he sobered up those dozen years. It was still half-full. He'd always left it in there, figuring his refusal to reach for it meant something back in the day. It probably did. Then. Now he just needed a drink. Nothing more complicated than that.

He wiped clean the inside of a coffee cup with a paper towel and poured it half full of the cheap booze. Price or quality meant nothing to a drunk. All he cared was that it was proofed enough to chisel the edges of the shame he felt, born of the foolishness of a lawman that lost his way.

As he drank the warm medicine for his soul he realized in all the years, sober or drunk, booze never made him feel ashamed. It was Wyoming. People drank. Since before the prairies were won—ripped away from those who owned them first—alcohol was always at hand.

Many felt that was still the way the government kept Native Americans in line on the reservations, by keeping them stocked with cheap liquor and nowhere to go and nothing to do.

Pruett could attest to the feral waste such a combination could wage across a man's will. Words like nowhere and nothing ate away at a person; ate away at him until he wasn't the same in the mirror in the mornings; gnawed at every part of him until all he wanted to do was drown himself in the misery and the booze.

He finished off the cup and put the bottle away. He suddenly felt like being at home; the home he and his wife had built together with their own hands, just as in the days of the old land—just as generations had done before them.

He wanted to be where the memory of his dead wife waited to cocoon him in a false sense that he could finally kick the habit for good, that everything would work out, justice would be served, and the world would then, for him anyway, stop spinning.

R.S. GUTHRIE

"A lady that knows me
affection she shows me
and a smile so easy and sweet.
The dreams that I've buried
the load that I've carried
Are some of the reasons I cheat."

Randy Travis,
Reasons I Cheat

Chapter 8

ONE DRY week that felt like a year.

How many years of sobriety have I pissed down the sewer this past month? Or was it two? Pruett wondered as he drank his second tonic water.

He sat at the Bar of the Willow Saloon, where he'd taken Ty into custody. Hanson, the lawyer, asked to meet him there.

"Sheriff Pruett," a voice declared from behind him.

Pruett turned to see the smiling face of J.W. Hanson.

"Sit," Pruett said. "Roland, whatever the man wants."

"Tullamore Dew," Hanson said.

"Heaven Hill," the sheriff corrected. "You want to talk to a gentleman, you drink bourbon. No goddamn Irish whisky swill. Besides, this way I get to smell it at least."

Hanson nodded to the bartender.

The two sat in silence for a time, Hanson screwing up the courage to say what he'd come to say. "You're aware of Wendy and me?"

"I'm aware," Pruett said. "You have any kids?"

"No," said Hanson.

"Married?"

"Once," Hanson said. "Divorced a number of years ago."

"Bethy and I almost divorced," Pruett said. "I was a hard drinker. Had a fling with this teacher in town. Stupid goddamn thing, but there it was. My daughter tell you about that?"

Hanson shook his head.

"Mostly why my daughter hates me," Pruett said. "That and the war."

"She doesn't hate you," Hanson said.

"Bethy forgave me. For both. Not like she should have. Took me a year to break it off with the teacher. Checked into a rehab place up in Cody. By the time I got back, teacher got herself fired. Bethy and I, we never talked about it again. I can't even remember that woman's name."

"We are never so defenseless against suffering as when we love," Hanson said.

"You dream that nonsense up yourself?"

"Freud," Hanson said, sipping on his whiskey. "Love ends up complicating things more than we'd hope, whatever you believe."

"Never felt like my love for Bethy was complicated. What did Freud say about following the angst in our loins?"

"A lot."

"How'd you get yourself divorced, Professor?"

"Guess."

"Now see, I like a man better when he speaks from experience. To hell with the quotes."

"Fair enough," Hanson acquiesced.

"It's hard," Pruett said. "Being worthy of a good woman's love."

"It's the *staying* worthy that challenges us."

"Another famous declaration?"

"J.W. Hanson," the professor said.

"Then I'll drink to it," Pruett said, lifting his glass of limewater.

Honey McIntyre came by the jail around eight-thirty P.M., while the sheriff was drinking a limewater with Ty's counsel. Zach Canter, youngest on staff was staffing the office.

"Uh, hello, ma'am," Canter said when she hobbled through the front door carrying a basket of fresh-baked bread on her elbow that immediately filled the place with the wonderful aroma of home. "What can I do for you?"

"Well I'd like to see my son," Honey said. "Give him some of his favorite pull-apart loaves. You, too, if you're hungry, young man."

"Uh, yes, ma'am. What I mean is, I'd be obliged for the bread, but I really shouldn't let you back with the prisoner. I mean, *Ty*. Visiting hours, well, they were over at six sharp. When the sheriff left."

Honey shuffled across the floor and looked up at Canter with emotionless eyes. "Your ma or pa have arthritis?" she said.

"No."

"You'd never have insulted a woman with such affliction who made the effort to come down here if they did."

"I'm sorry, ma'am. I guess it might be all right. For a couple of minutes is all."

"It was the bread, wasn't it?" Honey said, her eyes suddenly full of the rainbow of motherly love.

"Guess so," Canter said. He grabbed the key ring and escorted Honey back to where Ty was lying on his cot. "Five minutes, okay?"

"That'll be fine," said Honey. "You enjoy that pull-apart."

When Canter was gone Honey pressed up against the cell bars. "Get up here and talk to your mother, Tyree."

Ty stood and walked across the eight by twelve cell, head hung low.

"I brung you your favorite sweet bread."

"And I appreciate it, Ma."

"Reminds a man of home, don't it?" she said. "Used to make it for you boys back in the day."

"Yes."

"Families don't stop being families with age. Message is, we stick together when it counts, don't we?"

"That's a notion I figured you forgot," Ty said, still not meeting her gaze.

"If these bars weren't 'tween us I'd whip your ass for such talk."

"Yes, ma'am," Ty said and accepted the warm bread.

"You sit and eat. But you think about whose side yer on."

"Tell me about her," Pruett said.

"I thought she was the love of my life. I've since decided there is no such thing," Hanson said.

"Maybe not for some. For me, there was only one."

"Did your wife accept you for who you are?" Hanson asked.

"And then some," Pruett said. "But for me, it was hard living up to her expectations."

"Sorry?"

"Bethy loved me pure. It was me who could never accept who I was."

"May I ask you something personal, Sheriff?"

"I'd say we've passed that marker," Pruett said.

"With all due respect to your wife departed, why would you stray from one who was the only light in your life?"

"I thought we were talking about love," Pruett said. "There's a lot of ways to give a man light."

"So yours was a physical weakness?"

"Not only. Jesse was more like me. Flawed. My wife, she was of the finest stock; all color and clarity. With Jesse it was more like giving in to my own self. I didn't have to live up to her."

"I thought you said you'd forgotten her name," Hanson said.

"Man's memory has a funny way of waking back up to join the party, doesn't it?"

"That it does."

"Mind telling me about *your* transgressions?" Pruett said.

"My wife and I married at thirty. When we met, I thought I'd found my other half. The thing is, marriages aren't challenged in the good years. Like a well-built bridge. You can stand on it, drive over it—it's sturdy, you can *feel that*. But when the hurricane comes, *that's* when the engineering gets tested. That's when you know if the stanchions are sunk deep enough; that's how the true tensile strength of love is measured."

"So what was your storm, Professor?"

"Same as yours. Thing is, I was unfaithful one time. One single time. And this woman, who loved me without condition, could not find it in her heart to forgive me."

"And so it ended."

"Brutally, I'm afraid. She has not spoken to me since."

"May I share an observation, all respect intended?" Pruett said.

"Like you said, we're long past such concerns," Hanson said, finishing his drink.

"We ain't built the same, us and the gentler sex. Wired differently. That said, if she really loved you, she'd have stayed. You said it yourself: the tensile got tested. It was found wanting. In the big scheme, you were likely better off, all things known."

"I've tried to convince myself of that very thing."

"How's that worked out for you then?" Pruett said.

"Until I met Wendy, not particularly well."

"Hmm," Pruett said.

"I love her," Hanson said, motioning for another glass.

Pruett turned and looked at him. "How the hell old *are* you?"

"Fifty-seven," Hanson told him.

"Jesus," Pruett said. "You fight in 'Nam?"

Hanson shook his head. "I was in school. Deferred. If not for the deferral, I probably would have skipped to Canada."

Pruett thought for a moment. "Time was I would have punched you for that. Called you a coward. No more. You were the smart one, Professor."

"Never really felt like that," said Hanson.

"War is not favorable to those who wage it," Pruett said. "A circular hell, Professor."

"Still, I have thought many times that I should have learned that lesson for myself," Hanson admitted.

"So it's love?" the sheriff said.

"Yes," Hanson said.

"You sure?"

"Hellacious love, Sheriff."

Pruett lifted his impotent glass. "Only kind."

Patrolman James Pruett loved his wife. The life they'd carved out in Wyoming was a good one, and Bethy was the kind of woman for whom men pined. But ten years of heavy drinking eroded the will. It made a man feel invincible, as if the laws of others applied not to him.

At fourteen, Wendy Pruett already questioned her father's merit as a man. More than most teens. She was idealistic, and he was a cop who fought in the unpopular war. So, like any good drunk, Pruett did what he could to screw it up even more.

Jesse Claremont taught seventh grade at Wind River Middle School. She was young and pretty and she spent as many nights at the Cowboy Bar as James Pruett. While Sam and Bethy were at home, Pruett got to know Jesse. First it was just drinks at the bar and friendly flirtation. But things progressed. Soon it was two or three nights a week, all the drinking at Jesse's tiny one bedroom house in town. The sex was good. It seemed to revitalize Pruett, but then—at that time in his life—he was bulletproof. His own disease convinced him he could have it all. The booze, Jesse, *and* his wonderful life at home.

Wind River, like most small towns, allowed very few secrets. And Pruett was a cop. He knew better than anyone how word traveled. Pruett ignored the obvious. He and Jesse carried on in what they convinced themselves was secret. Until one night Pruett's daughter confronted him, standing stoically at the foot of his mistress's bed.

"You fucking shit," Pruett's only child had said. She did not cry; she would not give her father the satisfaction. But it was the last thing she said to him.

Wendy Steele waited nervously for her father. The Wrangler Cafe was teeming with men and women loading up on breakfast and coffee before jobs interrupted their days. Sheriff Pruett walked in and found her in the back corner of the restaurant. He waved, removed his hat, and tried to make his way through the crowd, stopping occasionally to shake a hand or pat a back.

"Sorry I'm behind," he said as he took a chair up next to her at the square table. He placed a checkered napkin in his lap.

"No worries," Wendy said. "I ordered us some coffee. Hope you still drink it."

"I do," said the sheriff. "Probably more than is healthy, though they change their minds on that daily it seems."

"True enough," she said as the coffee arrived.

"Morning, Sheriff," the server said.

"Angie. Keeping you jumping, I see," Pruett said.

"Oh yeah," Angie Hittle said, looking around the room. "Since the boom, we can't empty the place. It's good seeing you, Wendy. You let me know when y'all are ready to order."

They drank their coffee and spoke politely.

"Town has changed a lot," Wendy said.

"Towns do. This one more than most, though."

"Not as quiet as it used to be."

"No," Pruett said.

"Jay says you talked the other night," Wendy said.

The sheriff nodded. "Yep. Nice enough guy."

"But," Wendy said.

"No buts. Nice enough guy. That's it."

Angie returned and took their orders.

"Can I ask you something?" Wendy said.

"You bet."

"All these years, did you even miss me?"

"Jesus, Wendy, what do you think?"

"You never called, never wrote. Mom did, sent cards. I don't even remember what your handwriting looks like, you know?"

"You left, Wendy. I know I screwed up, but you remember, I tried to get you to talk to me. Even after you were gone. After a while…"

"After a while you gave up?"

"After a while, I guess my pride said I wasn't going to grovel anymore. I got sober."

"What about the twelve steps? Amends and all that?"

"I wrote you a letter. I could just never bring myself to send it. You hurt me, too, girl. There was a time you were everything to me."

"You can't lay it all on me like that, Sheriff."

"No, I can't. And I'm not. Just telling you where I was at."

"Fair enough," Wendy said.

The breakfast arrived and they ate in silence. Afterward, Pruett asked if she'd ride with him to the town park.

"We used to sit on this bench," Pruett said, as they sat down in front of Pine Creek.

"Better days," Wendy said.

"I can't make excuses, Wendy. I can't change what I did to you or to your mother. I'd ask you to forgive me, like she did."

"I will. I mean, I guess I have, Sheriff. These past few months have put a lot in perspective. I've missed you…"

Pruett put his arm around her narrow shoulders and she leaned into him. It felt good. Like they'd never parted. She fit perfectly against him, just as her mother had; it was as if they were both grooved to live permanently at his side.

"There ain't nothing I can do
Or nothing I can say
That folks don't criticize me
But I'm going to do
Just as I want to anyway"

Billie Holiday/Freddie King,
Ain't Nobody's Business

Chapter 9

THE RECORDS were not that hard to find; a person only had to be looking. And it didn't hurt to know who to ask. Ty McIntyre would never have looked. Rory counted on that fact. A fortune split three ways was not only more lucrative but a hell of a way to stick it to the man in the world most like him.

The idea came to Pruett when Ty said something about blood being more important than money.

Why would Ty's grandfather, Willy McIntyre, take any chances with the inheritance?

Normally, not a big stretch. But Pruett happened to know the deceased McIntyre employed a damn fine lawyer; he knew it because Willy used her several times in land disputes with the county.

It occurred to Pruett there was little chance that Beulah Jorgensen—who in addition to being Town Attorney did plenty of private work on the side—ignored the significance of surface versus mineral rights.

This meant that either Willy or Rory McIntyre intentionally cheated Ty out of his birthright. Pruett knew two things for certain:

Willy McIntyre loved Ty fiercely.

And Beulah Jorgensen, cantankerous as she was, would not be party to something so deliberately heinous.

That left Rory.

Rory and Ty never saw eye-to-eye. Ty was too strong-willed, too much like his old man. They'd fought openly. Physically. It just never occurred to Pruett that the old man would take it that far. And if Ty had found out...

Pruett brought a pair of old-fashioned donuts and a steaming coffee from the local bakery to Gert Lundergaard, County Clerk. He didn't need bribery to get anything from Gert, he simply knew what she loved, and he liked to indulge her. Gert had been there for him during the long haul months after Bethy's death, the one person in town with whom he could share the terrible fear he felt climbing into an empty bed each night. Gert lost her husband of fifty-two years the winter before, to cancer.

"Morning, sweetie," Pruett said, handing the bounty to Gert.

"You are a fine man, Sheriff James," Gert said. "You know my sweet spot."

"I need a favor," Pruett said.

"No need to say so," Gert said, pulling out a fresh donut. "Just tell me."

"Need all the land records and the will from the McIntyre estate."

"Popular files," Gert said.

"How so?"

"Beulah Jorgensen. She was in here last week, reviewing the same. This have to do with the trial?"

"Maybe," Pruett said.

"Give me a few minutes," Gert said, and disappeared into the file room behind her station.

Funny thing about dishonest people, Pruett thought as he read through the official documents—one being the Last Will and Testament of William Joshua McIntyre: *Very few are as swift as you see 'em in the movies.*

But there was no horseplay Pruett could see in the original disposition of the estate. It was clear how the property was to be divided and nothing was said about mineral rights separately.

The document also named Rory the executor of the estate. As such, all future proceeds would funnel through the father and down to the grandsons. It was unlikely Ty even attended the reading of the will, much less would have understood any of the legalese. Rory would easily have been able to satisfy Ty with a chunk of property, divided just as the will demanded.

The mineral rights issue was happening all over the state; perhaps rather than malfeasance the McIntyres really had been caught in the unintended inequity all over the state of Wyoming in the gas boom.

Pruett frowned. Something was wrong. Beulah would have known about the mineral rights—she was too bright to miss something like that—and Will McIntyre would never have settled for his favorite grandson being left empty handed.

The land dispute of the McIntyre's was gossip around town, but Beulah Jorgensen would have *had* to know that the gossip was more or less true. She would have *known* that Ty's own ignorance was being used against him. Or something worse…

The sheriff's next stop was to the Town Attorney's office. Beulah was in, preparing for opening arguments. Pruett sat down hard in the chair facing her across the lacquered desk.

"Help you, Sheriff?" Jorgensen said without looking up.

"Sure can. You can tell me how it is that the City Attorney came to defraud one of her own constituency."

Jorgensen set her pen down and looked up at Pruett, her eyes dark and unaffected. "Slander is a serious offense, particularly for an officer of the law," she said. A crack in her voice betrayed what Pruett had suspected. She was hiding *something*.

"You had to know what was going on. You would have advised Will about the potential for income from mineral rights on certain parcels, yet the will itself says nothing. It doesn't address a *thing*. You expect me to believe Will McIntyre wouldn't have made provisions for Ty? You also had to know it was only a matter of time before Ty found out. You might as well have loaded the goddamn gun yourself, Beulah."

There was a silence. Jorgensen was obviously choosing her response, going over in her mind what the sheriff knew and how much was just fishing. In the end, she must have decided Pruett had dug up the documents.

"After the will was read, Rory met with me in private. Not unusual, since I represented his father. He retained my services, that's all. Totally legal."

"And because you were his attorney, unless you had *direct* knowledge…"

"Unless I had direct knowledge of any legal malfeasance, not only was I under no obligation to report my client, I was under a code of ethics *not to*."

"So you're saying what? That you screwed up and never told Ty's grandfather about the rights underground?"

"You know I can't discuss any more of this with you," she said. "I am a lawyer and my clients have a lawful expectation of my silence."

"At the very least, this is a goddamn conflict of interest," Pruett said. "You are the prosecutor. *And* you represent the father of the accused—a potentially intended *victim*."

"This is none of your concern, Sheriff."

"My wife died because of all this, you fucking bitch."

Jorgensen looked up, pointing the pen at him. "You watch yourself, Sheriff. You fucking watch what you say to me. And get the hell out of my office."

Pruett stood and stared at her. He'd never considered Jorgensen anything other than a stalwart when it came to her profession. He had respected her. Now he felt as if he were tugging at the fray on a ball of twine. There was more here. A lot more. That much he'd swear to.

He turned and left, returned to the County Clerk.

"Gerty," Pruett said.

"Yeah, hon?"

"A man wanted to dig up some dirt on a person, this day and age. Where would he start?"

To Pruett the computer on his desk was useful only in blocking him from view. A privacy shield, little more. He barely emailed.

"Honey, you have come to the right place."

Gerty Lundergaard knew the Internet. She showed Pruett where, for less than fifty bucks, he could more or less put together a timeline of a person's life. For a few hundred, he could pull Beulah Jorgensen's bank records.

What he found was not so much shocking as it was depressing. Pruett loved Wind River and his hold on the belief that his town was immune to the debasement, greed, and outright cheating that had captured much of the country had once been strong. The discovery that Beulah Jorgensen had made several substantially-sized deposits since the time that Will McIntyre died was just too damned coincidental, and it severed his belief in that small town immunity forever.

The Town Attorney's office was really only three attorneys: Beulah Jorgensen, Miles Stanton, and Shelly Delgado. Pruett had no way of being certain how deep the conspiracy went, but he doubted the other two attorneys were involved. The chances of carrying out a crime diminished exponentially as one added members to the operation. It also lowered the take.

Pruett called Shelly Delgado. Shelly was a divorcee with two children. Stanton was married with three children and a mortgage. Pruett just didn't see motive in either of them, but Shelly Delgado lived small, and her ex, Joe Delgado, was an oil baron who paid her a handsome alimony settlement each month. Unlikely she would have anything to do with fraud for profit.

"City attorney's office," Delgado answered.

"Shell, it's James Pruett."

"Sheriff Pruett. How are you doing?"

"I'm well. Doing fine. Listen, Shell, you have time for a lunch date?"

"A date? Damn, Sheriff, you know how to talk to a lady."

"Just the two of us, if you know what I mean? Professional-like," he said.

"Sure, sweetie. Nothing Beulah needs to know about."

Shelly was bright. Pruett was counting on it.

They met at Lyman's Pub, a new bistro on the edge of town with a private patio.

"Were you involved at all in the McIntyre estate settlement," Pruett asked.

"No," Delgado replied. "Beulah does her side representation. We're encouraged not to do the same ourselves."

"That seems fair," the sheriff said and drank his iced tea.

"Life, love, and war," Shelly said.

"You've never struck me as the type to cause yourself debits in order to gain upward mobility."

"I'm not a mover and a shaker, that what you are trying to say?"

"Guess so," Pruett said thinking how good a cold microbrew would taste.

"I love the law," she responded. "Always have. I figure as long as I am practicing, I'm doing what I was meant to be doing. I don't need the moniker on the door."

"I think Beulah is dirty," Pruett said, laying it there in the middle of them. "I can't prove anything as definite yet, but there is a strange and befouled undercurrent running in your office."

Delgado said nothing.

"That doesn't draw outrage?" Pruett said. "No indignation even?"

"We're talking about my career now, Pruett," she said slowly. "Right or wrong, I really don't warm up to the idea of being unemployed. Not much lawyering going on in this little town, in case you hadn't noticed. Mine is a pretty good gig for a small town girl."

"Not for one with a love of the law," he said.

"Maybe not," Shelly said. "But we each make a sacrifice. Sometimes more than one."

"I have suspicions," Pruett said. "I wanted to bring it to you first. If you have no interest in justice, then I'll go to Jackson. Or anywhere else in the state. I could even go to the Feds. I wanted to give you the chance, if you were willing."

"You know what this will do for the defense, right?"

Pruett knew. He also knew Delgado was right. Everyone makes sacrifices. To put Beulah Jorgensen under indictment in the very conspiracy that started the wheels of murder headed toward his wife would be to hand the defense the case. He could be freeing the man who murdered his beloved.

"I know what it means," Pruett said. "I also know what Bethy would have me do, were she able to say so."

"Beulah has a place where she keeps her personal files," Delgado said. "I mean *personal*. As in, hidden. She's an oaf. Thinks no one is the wiser. You tell me what you have and maybe I'll have a looksee into that private stock of paperwork."

The next person to visit was J.W. Hanson. Pruett now knew of Ty's intent to confess to the crime, and though he knew Hanson would try to talk the cowboy out of doing such a thing, Pruett figured the lawyer would be more motivated if he knew what train was barreling down the track. Pruett found Hanson at his hotel room, with Wendy.

"A minute of your time," Pruett said, touching the tip of his hat and smiling at his daughter.

"Sure," said Hanson. The two walked out into the parking lot of the Shady Day hotel.

"I know what Ty's planning tomorrow," Pruett said.

"He mentioned that he told you," said Hanson. "Though I am sure that makes you a happy man, I am trying to convince him otherwise."

"I figured," said Pruett. "Ty can be stubborn."

"On that much, we agree," Hanson said.

"I have some information that might make your argument a little more convincing."

"Sorry, *more* convincing?" Hanson said.

"I'm an officer of the law, Professor. This is a matter of due process, and of justice. I'm not interested in anything else," Pruett said.

"My apologies," Hanson allowed. "You were saying?"

"Beulah Jorgensen does some business on the side. She represented both Will *and* Rory McIntyre."

"She disclosed these relationships in discovery," Hanson said.

"Did she disclose she's been taking sizeable payoffs from Rory McIntyre since the death of his father and the reading of the McIntyre will?"

Hanson stood there, incredulous, his chiseled features trying their best to twist themselves into a look of surprise. "You have *proof* of this allegation?"

"I can't prove yet where the payoffs came from, but they're big— too big for a Town Attorney—and they began three days after the reading of the will," Pruett said.

"Jesus."

"Shelly Delgado is looking into some files Beulah keeps on the side, see if there's anything of interest there," Pruett said.

"Why are you doing this?" he said. "I mean, you know what Ty intends to do."

"I want what's right and fair, Professor. My own daughter has never really believed that about me. Not sure I've always believed it. But it's what I want."

"You should know something," Hanson said. "In the spirit of full disclosure."

Pruett looked at him.

"This is a breach," the professor said. "But I feel under the circumstances I can trust you with this information."

"Shoot," Pruett said.

"We've already met with Jorgensen. Ty refuses to take any plea arrangement. In fact, he is asking for the maximum penalty."

"And Jorgensen is agreeable?" Pruett said.

"I'd describe her as *giddy*," Hanson remarked.

The hatred in Pruett burned. Fuck it, he thought. Time to pull harder on the fray.

"The sky is falling
with the ash and mud
They gotta make a promise
yeah, blood to blood
So shut the door
and then slowly turn around
And now you know
you can't make a sound."

Roseanne Cash,
Burn Down This Town

Chapter 10

"YOU KNEW all of this," Hanson asked his client.

"I knew," Ty said.

Hanson was sitting on the cot; Ty McIntyre's back was to his attorney, and he leaned languidly on the bars of his cell.

"How did you find out?" Hanson said.

"My old man let it slip. He was drunk. Told me he didn't want to go to his grave not having told me how good he screwed me. Said I'd never be able to prove it."

"I have some news that may change how you feel about all this," Hanson said.

"Ain't nothin' ever going to change how I feel about all this," Ty said. "Not ever."

"I think Beulah Jorgensen was involved," Hanson said. "I think there may have been tampering with your grandfather's will."

"Don't matter," said McIntyre.

"She can't prosecute you, Ty. Not if we can find the proof we're after. She'll be disbarred and criminally charged. Your old man, too. And I doubt seriously if the City Attorney's office is going to want to go full tilt on a new trial. I think you can plead out to manslaughter two. Maybe negligent death. You could get probation with time served, considering the injustice."

"Told you what I wanted you to do. Just need you to do it, lawyer man."

"Ty, as your attorney..."

"Just fucking *do it*," Ty hissed.

The plea hearing began at ten A.M. At nine o'clock, Pruett met with Hanson in an anteroom, before the proceedings began.

"You tried to talk him out of it?" Pruett said. "Pleading guilty, I mean?"

Hanson nodded. "The determination of that man is as astounding as it is problematic."

"This is all wrong," Pruett said.

"I'd think you of all people would feel just the opposite."

"There's more behind this. We've just been pickin' at scabs—there's a lot more bleeding to come, I believe," Pruett said.

"It's within my ability to withdraw as counsel under such a plea. It would add some time to the process, but it's very unlikely to change the outcome."

"Let him plead guilty," Pruett proclaimed. He was tired and felt old as time. He wasn't sure he wanted to know the truth anymore. If Ty had killed Bethy, why shouldn't he just say so?

Pruett sat in the crowded gallery, behind the defendant's table. Deputies Munney and Baptiste stood at opposing sides of the courtroom and Zach Canter guarded the door. It was standing room only. The court granted media access, but only at the rear of the courtroom and only as space permitted. He stated there would be no camping out—that the courtroom doors opened at eight o'clock each morning and that the first half hour was designated for family, friends, and townsfolk, in that order. The press was to be allowed the final fifteen minutes between eight forty-five and nine to gather in the rear of the courtroom.

"All rise," Baptiste bellowed as the Honorable Bridger C. Butler entered the courtroom. He was shorter than Pruett remembered.

"Be seated," Butler said, reviewing some paperwork on the bench.

He looked up, nodding at the prosecutor, who was standing already.

"Beulah Jorgensen, Your Honor. From the Town Prosecutor's office, representing the State of Wyoming."

"Ms. Jorgensen," the judge said. He looked to the defendant's table.

Hanson stood. "J.W. Hanson, Your Honor. Representing the accused."

"Mr. Hanson," Judge Butler said. "Before we begin, I wish to say a few words to the courtroom. It is not within my domain to lessen the sensational nature of the charges in this case, nor am I inclined to issue any directives to the press insofar as any gag orders. I am a staunch believer in our ancestors' intent to protect the freedom of speech. That said, I would ask that all reporting heretofore be as accurate and without intentional drama as is prudent. Otherwise, it is *well* within my power to exclude all media from these premises."

Without asking for anyone's acquiescence, Butler turned to the defense.

"Mr. Hanson, how does your client plead?"

J.W. Hanson nodded to Ty, who stood up.

"Guilty, Judge," Ty McIntyre said.

Butler looked as if he'd swallowed a fly. He turned toward the Prosecution's table. "Ms. Jorgensen, is there an agreement between these parties of which the court is unaware?"

"No, Your Honor. There is no plea agreement."

"Counsel, approach," Butler said, waving them in.

When Hanson and Jorgensen were in front of him, the judge twisted the small microphone to the right and covered it from view with his right hand. He addressed J.W. Hanson quietly.

"Mr. Hanson, this is a bit irregular. Truth told, we would have saved the State of Wyoming significant tax dollars were a simple confession presented upon arrest. With all respect, you do realize your client is charged with an offense that will result in him being sentenced to the most severe punishment allowable by law."

"I understand, Your Honor."

"He will be put to *death*, sir."

"My client is aware, Judge. He makes this plea against my advice and despite my sternest objection."

Butler turned to Beulah Jorgensen. "Ms. Jorgensen. Under the circumstances, is there leeway in the severity of the charges at hand? Under Wyoming law, a conviction for a premeditative act such as this leaves me little room for mercy. None, actually."

"The State is not willing to lessen the charge, Your Honor."

"Return," Butler said, obviously annoyed.

"Mr. McIntyre," the judge began when counsel had returned to their respective tables. "Do you understand the nature of the charge levied against you—that charge being murder in the first degree with aggravating circumstances?"

"Yessir," Ty said, his head bowed.

"Please speak up for the record, Mr. McIntyre," Butler said.

"Yes, I understand the charges against me," Ty said, loudly this time.

"For the record, do you understand that a plea of 'guilty' will result in you being sentenced to death? I need you to understand the gravity of what you are pleading, and more importantly, sir, the seriousness of the sentence that will be imposed upon you."

Ty McIntyre looked directly into the eyes of the judge, annunciating each word:

"I am guilty of murder, Judge. What I wish is to receive full sentence for what I done."

Butler held Ty's gaze for a few moments, perhaps looking for a lack of surety. He apparently found none. "I assume you make this plea of your own accord, Mr. McIntyre. That you are under no obligation or duress?"

"No, sir. No duress. I admit what I done freely."

Butler turned again to the Prosecution. "Ms. Jorgensen?"

Beulah paused, staring down at the blank notebook before her on the table. "The State opposes the defendant's plea, Your Honor."

Butler drew back perceptibly. "Excuse me?"

"Based on the nineteen ninety-seven decision in the case State of Wyoming versus Roy W. Montgomery, Judge; a capital murder case. The Prosecution has the right to decline any plea, even—and under some circumstances, *particularly due to*—a guilty one."

She reached in her satchel and removed a printed sheet of paper. She read aloud: "From Judge Henry Reinwald's written decision:

'In response to a charge of murder with special circumstances, wherein the death penalty is sought; if the court believes there is substantive cause to suggest the accused harbors a 'death wish', i.e. makes his or her plea under self-serving or suicidal auspices, the court may require a 'not guilty' plea in expectation of a trial by a jury of peers'."

Judge Butler sat, transfixed.

"The decision was upheld, Your Honor," Jorgensen said. "The jury found Montgomery guilty, and having received a death sentence, the defense even petitioned the Appellate Court to set aside the verdict and accept Montgomery's original plea. The court upheld the decision and was *adamant* in denying the defendant's plea of 'guilty' and refused to set aside the verdict, based on the grounds that were it to accept the *original* plea in place of the verdict, the court would be condoning the man's wish to die."

Butler looked back to J.W. Hanson. Then again to Jorgensen. His expression was that of a cornered animal, wary of the next step. He eventually found his poker face and addressed the room:

"Contingent on my review of Ms. Jorgensen's precedent, this court denies the defendant's 'guilty' plea and enters one of 'not guilty'. Opening arguments begin tomorrow, Tuesday, and nine A.M."

Hanson did not object.

The thunder of Butler's gavel was the only sound in the room.

Sheriff Pruett met with Hanson after the plea hearing.

"A stroke of genius," Hanson said. "Professionally speaking, it's almost a shame you're going to take that woman down."

"To hell with that woman," Pruett said. "Even a crazy dog outsmarts the fox once in a while."

"What have you heard from Ms. Delgado?"

"Nothing," Pruett said. "I planned to drop by the office after the hearing. You care to join me?"

Beulah Jorgensen was not gloating. In fact, she was not present at the Town Attorney's office when Pruett and J.W. Hanson arrived. But neither was Shelly Delgado.

"She didn't show up today," Miles Stanton told them.

"She didn't call?" the sheriff asked.

"No, but that's not surprising. Her two kids are always coming down with something. She takes her work home," Stanton said.

"Cold feet?" Hanson said as they drove to the Blackstone subdivision east of town.

"Can't say," Pruett said. "She wasn't thrilled about the news I gave her. Maybe Stanton's right and her kids have the flu."

Pruett knocked on the door of Shelly Delgado's home, a large log house she inherited from her ex-husband in the divorce settlement.

No answer. Pruett walked around and looked in the cathedral-height front glass, but could see no movement in the house.

"I'll drop you at the courthouse," Pruett said. "Figure I might just drop by Joe Delgado's place out on the golf course."

Shelly's ex was home and invited Pruett in.

"Morning, Sheriff," he said, offering some fresh coffee, which Pruett accepted.

"Wondering if you know where Shelly is today," Pruett said.

"Don't keep tabs on her, Sheriff. Something I should know about?"

"No. Just needed to talk to her. She didn't show up at work so we figured she was home with the kids."

"Kids are in school," Delgado said, sipping at the black coffee. "They're with me all week."

"Hmm," Pruett said. "Thanks for your time, Joe."

Back at Shelly Delgado's house, Sheriff Pruett walked around to the back yard and stepped through the two-rail fence. The rear door to the garage was unlocked, so he opened it and slipped in. Shelly's Nissan was parked in there. Pruett walked past the car and checked the engine. Cold. He turned the knob to the house door; it too was unlocked. So he entered.

The house was like a palatial cabin. The kitchen was all granite, with tall pine cabinets offset by stainless steel appliances. Pruett walked through the kitchen and into the high ceiling living room. There was a cup of cold coffee on a table. Also on the table were what looked like Shelly's hand-carry brief, a blank legal tablet, and two pens. A laptop power cable lay next to the tablet, unplugged.

"Shelly," Pruett called out. The fact that he'd not thought until now to call for her caused a chill to creep up his spine. He removed the Smith and Wesson pistol from its holster. "Hello. Anyone?"

Pruett moved cautiously toward the back of the house. As he turned a corner, he saw one of Shelly Delgado's bare legs protruding from the back bedroom, lying still on the hardwood floor. The Sheriff quickly made sure the rooms were clear and approached the office.

Blood spatter fanned up the log wall on one side. There was a large amount of thick, dark blood pooled around her head. He reached for Shelly's neck. No pulse. The body was already cold, a hole in her head on one side. Pruett guessed she'd been killed the night before.

The sheriff rubbed his eyes and holstered his weapon. His peaceful Wyoming town was starting to feel like a war zone.

"Gonna put the world
away for a minute
Pretend I don't live in it
Sunshine gonna
wash my blues away."

Zac Brown,
Knee Deep

Chapter 11

PRUETT HAD once wondered to himself, years ago: *where does it come from, this duty good cops feel bound to—this sacred responsibility to speak for the dead?*

He knew it was erroneous to say it was inherent in the job; that all law enforcement personnel felt this way. Some cops—patrol officers, detectives, deputies, agents, marshals—they worked the job just as any other professional: they clocked in, did their jobs, and they clocked out.

Survived the day. Made it home. Performed their duty as stated in the job description—no more, no less.

So the feeling did not simply *come with the territory*. Such noble ideals did not germinate in every man or woman who signed up for the job. For the really good cops, it seemed to Pruett, it was not a matter of applying for a position—the job, well, it found *them*. As if the duty was a part of their DNA waiting to be discovered.

No cop—good, bad, or otherwise—began their career thinking: *I will stand up for the deceased.*

The dead man.

Those murdered girls.

A bullet-riddled gang-banger.

A battered wife finally slain.

At some point in the job, however, the sense of duty changed. For many, that moment drove them to retire—to find a different career. For Pruett—and for so many other cops—it was the day they realized the dead had no one left to speak for them. They were victims who no longer had a voice and someone had to stand up on their behalf.

For Pruett, the case that changed him forever was a multiple homicide in the second year of his first term as Sublette County Sheriff.

A panel truck full of dead Mexicans, left in the middle of Wyoming to rot.

Men. Women. Teens.

And younger.

Pruett had listened to the tales of his ancestors—stories that described cruel, sometimes unbelievable acts that occurred in the "winning of the West".

The prairie, it bled.

But it seemed to Pruett that the bloodletting at the core of those old stories—struggles between the white man and the Indian, the outlaw against the honorable, the harsh elements against anything that crawled or thirsted—scurrilous as bloodletting always is, still represented a kind of progress toward the future. Not always fair; not always judicious. Unavoidable human suffering in the building of a country; sacrifice—both just and unjust—in the construct of a nation.

But the carnage Pruett and his deputy were to discover in the sealed rear cargo bay of the rusted white truck—the wanton disregard for life—did not serve to build anything. Such atrocity had the capacity to destroy the faith of good inside every man and woman.

"I can smell it already," said Deputy Fred Morgan as Pruett drove the old county Suburban over the tangled sagebrush. Morgan worked under Sheriff Pruett the first year and a half, taking the call from a rancher who'd been headed to town for a week's supply of groceries and reported the old panel truck, parked several hundred feet off the dirt road. The rusted white Dodge was halfway into a small draw, cantering slightly westward, toward the now setting sun. The rancher had called, in part, because of the stench.

"Put on your kerchief," Pruett said.

He and Deputy Morgan had soaked two bandanas in gasoline earlier, anticipating the supplication of flesh to the sweltering, airless heat—bodies having waited for them there in the brushy arroyo for days or weeks.

At fifty feet, the horseflies sounded like an army of motorbikes. Enough blood had run from under the closed rear door that the loamy ground surrounding the vehicle was stained the color of molasses.

"Cut it," Pruett said to Morgan, who carried bolt-cutters.

Morgan clipped the padlock that withheld the horror on the other side of the door. Both men left their pistols holstered. Whatever evil had been in this place had locked the door from the outside. Pruett reached down and pulled the sliding door up.

The rush of decay was too much for the gasoline rags and the two cops were forced to backpedal ten or fifteen feet. Morgan fell to his knees, coughing, and emptied his stomach on the dusty earth.

Pruett gathered himself and walked forward. The carnage was unspeakable. Bodies lay in a twisted heap of decomposition. The sheriff could see immediately it was mass murder. The men's heads each exhibited a single gunshot wound to the head, as did all the male teenagers. Younger children, teen girls, and women had been strung together in twos or in threes, twine tied about their throats to cut off the airways and to keep them from struggling as their killers assaulted them.

It took thirty-eight hours for the medical examiner, six members of the Sheriff's department, five officers from the Wyoming State Patrol, four EMTs, and several volunteers from town, to move and bag the bodies. The crime scene was preserved as best they knew how.

But it wasn't the egregiousness of the murders that changed young Sheriff Pruett. It was the facts of the case that settled him at his core.

Bud Havenstead was well known and well liked. He and his family had run cattle south of Wind River, in Rock Valley, since there were but ten post office boxes for all the mail in town.

But ranching in the twenty-first century had become a crapshoot. Bud had lost his tits more times over in years than he cared to count. And the drying up of the money was hurting his boys, too. They'd been pulled from the rodeo circuit two years running, and for thick, surly, hardened young men, rodeo was the only thing that burned off the angst.

Turned out Buck, the oldest boy, had worked out a deal with a couple of coyotes from Mexico—met them when they delivered several bulls to an outfit in Nagel, Arizona near the end of two thousand and one. For a hundred dollars a head, plus expenses, Buck would drive a panel truck full of illegals up through Wyoming and Montana, and drop them off near the border of Canada.

Buck Havenstead made ten runs a year, right up to the final trip—the one just after the coyote boss in Arizona discovered Buck was running his mouth in a Nagel bar about the business.

Sheriff Pruett found Bud Havenstead's oldest son at the bottom of the heap of bodies. They never did find his head.

Until that day James Pruett had believed in his heart that there were havens where the things that walked in his nightmares never visited. Like small towns in the middle of the rugged Rocky Mountains. But that day a Sheriff learned that lawlessness and evil are a human inherency; that you can travel to any of the four corners of the land, move to a quaint, peaceful Wyoming town, hide even, within the four borders of your home.

But evil will come.

Pruett learned that day, it always does.

He also learned that day that if his office did not champion the dead—if *he* did not—no one would.

"There's something I think you should hear," Hanson said to the sheriff. He'd just come from his client's cell.

"From the prisoner," Pruett said.

Hanson nodded.

"Kinda goes against the whole protected conversation thing, don't it?"

"My client has pled guilty and is asking for the death penalty to be applied to himself," Hanson said. "Under the circumstances I think I can chance a breach of ethics. This is important."

Pruett followed the lawyer back to the jail.

"Tell him what you told me," Hanson said to Ty.

Ty rubbed the back of his skull. "Dryin' out has give me back some of the memories from that night."

"Memories," Pruett said.

"Yep. I remember why it was I went out to the ranch. I was lookin' for Pa."

Pruett turned to Hanson. "Not exactly worthy of the evening news."

"I went out there," Ty interrupted, "because that son-of-a-bitch tried to kill me."

"Rory tried to kill you?" Pruett said.

"As sure as the day is long he tried to put a bullet in my skull."

"It's more than a little hard to believe you are just remembering all this right now," Pruett said.

"I tied a helluva rope on that night. After my Pa tried to put me in the grave, that is. At first, I wasn't goin' to do nothin'. But the drunker I got the madder I got."

"Any reason you can think of your pa might be driven to murder you? That's a steep accusation, Ty."

"He must've found out I knew about the swindle."

"What swindle?"

"The one got cooked up with that fuckin' lawyer. Jorgensen. She's been takin' the old man's money for years to screw me over."

Pruett dragged a chair across the cold concrete. "Tell me the whole thing. The attempted murder first," he said to his prisoner.

"Whatever I can remember," Ty said.

"That'll have to do."

Ty gave the sheriff a pretty tall tale. Said he was getting drunk in his own ranch house when he thought he heard a vehicle driving up the road. He went outside but no one was there. No headlights either. So the old cowpoke went back to drinking.

A few minutes later Ty heard a floorboard creak and turned just in time to see the muzzle of a Colt 32-20 Army revolver pointed at the back of his head. He was pretty drunk by then but he managed to put a forearm into the side of the barrel and knock the cannon a few inches sideways before it went off. The concussion knocked Ty sideways and he fell out of his chair. He scrambled to his feet the best he could, but when his vision cleared, there was no one there—just the acrid smell of cordite, hanging there in the air like a shirt on the clothesline. He stumbled out to the front but it was moonless and he couldn't see anyone. He did, however, hear an engine start up in the distance and a pair of headlights swing wide and away, the vehicle roaring back the way it had come.

"So that's when you loaded up for bear and drove to your pa's ranch?" Sheriff Pruett said.

"No. I drank several more shots first."

"But you never did see who it was."

"Saw the gun. You think I don't know my old man's pistola?"

"You don't know it was him. Could've been someone else took Rory's gun. Could've been a close match. You didn't see *anything?*"

"I smelt him," Ty said flatly. "I'd know that stink water anywhere."

Pruett looked at Hanson, who shrugged his narrow shoulders. "Legally? Probably not enough for a warrant. Not with the booze involved."

Ty turned and lay down on the cot.

"Bullet went straight through the drywall," he said. "Probably stuck in the wood beyond."

Pruett turned and walked down the corridor, J.W. Hanson close behind.

"I'm coming with you," Hanson said.

The old Suburban bounced and rattled its way down the washed out road to Ty McIntyre's place.

"With a slug," Hanson said, "and Ty's testimony, we should be able to get a warrant for Rory's property."

Pruett grunted. He didn't like where this thing was headed. Ty had already confessed, or at least had tried to plead guilty. And now he said he remembered doing it. No matter what they found, Bethy was still dead.

He wanted a drink.

Bad.

They arrived at Ty's house. A few stray cats scattered, but there were no other signs of life. The ranch house was more of a cabin, with dilapidated, uneven logs and large, incongruous patches of mud holding the thing together.

"Ty said he was sitting here, in this recliner," Pruett said. "And that the shooter came from behind, over there."

He pointed to a back hallway. Hanson went down the short corridor and called out: "There's a back entrance. In the laundry."

Pruett quickly figured the bullet's trajectory and looked over to the void, peeling wall. There were no pictures or other ornaments to distract the eye, so the hole stood out amongst the curling paint, bug smears, and tobacco grime.

The sheriff used his buck knife to cut a square access hole and pointed to his toolbox.

"Hand me that flashlight," he said to Hanson.

It took him a few minutes, but Pruett found the crushed slug—its widened butt protruding from the rotting wood behind the drywall. He carefully dug it from the pliable wood and deposited it in an evidence bag.

"Let's go hassle a judge."

Bridger Butler signed the search warrant for the Rory McIntyre ranch in the small office of the Wagon Wheel Inn, where he was lodged.

"A bit irregular for the sitting judge to issue a warrant regarding his own case," said Butler. "But this is Wyoming. You aren't going to get another judge to do one over the phone, now are you?"

Pruett called in all of his deputies. "We're looking for Rory's .32," Pruett said. "Plus any pairs of tan work gloves we see. Ty said Rory was wearing them."

They took the Suburban, since it could carry the lot of them. Hanson came, too, against the sheriff's better sense.

"What the hell you and the cavalry doin' here," Rory said when he answered the door. "It's supper time."

"Warrant to search the premises," Pruett told him and handed him the paper.

The deputies did not wait to be invited in, pushing past the old rancher.

"Ma'am," said Canter to Honey McIntyre, who was standing next to a small Lucite table with a nice pork chop dinner getting cold in the middle of it.

"You want to save us some time, Rory? Tell us where you keep your Colt .32?" Pruett said.

"It's in the holster, hanging on the bed post. Where it always is. You fuckin' need me to draw you a map?"

"Got it," said Mel Munney a few moments later.

"Where you keep your work gloves?" the sheriff said.

"Christ Jesus," Rory said. "What the hell is this about, Pruett?"

"Where are they, Rory?"

"Where you think my gloves is? Outside, with the tractor. I was fixin' fence. You seen it with your own eyes."

Pruett motioned to Baptiste. "You got more than one pair, Rory?"

"No I don't. I wear through one, I get another. What else?"

"You need to come with us," Pruett said. "There are questions need answering."

"What questions?" Rory said, low and cold.

"Let's go," Pruett said.

Rory sat in the station break room, drinking lukewarm coffee, then Pruett sat came in and told him what they knew.

"Never went to Ty's place," Rory said. "Haven't been out there in two, maybe three years."

"Your gloves have powder residue on them, Rory. Means you were wearing them when you shot your pistol, just like Ty remembers."

"Ha, that'll be the day. That drunk don't remember where his own pecker's at most the time."

"You want to explain the residue?"

"I've shot that gun a hundred times with my gloves on. Gets cold around here, 'case you ain't noticed."

"What were you shooting at most recently?" Pruett said.

"Sage hens."

"You get any?"

"Nope."

"Bad shot?"

"What?"

"You're a bad shot. I mean, missed the sage hens, Ty's still alive. Poor shot, I guess is the correct vernacular."

"Screw you."

Pruett slid his chair closer to the table and leaned in. "I want to talk about your coat and hat again," the sheriff said.

"First it's gloves. Now it's my hat. You want I should show you my undergarments, too?"

"I just can't see Bethy going for your coat when her own was right there," Pruett said. "And the hat? No way."

"I told you how it went down."

"Well that's not how Honey remembers it."

Rory looked cockeyed for the first time during the interview. "What did that woman tell you?"

"She says you jumped right up and offered 'em to her."

"So what? So I don't remember every fuckin' detail."

Something in Rory's countenance changed then, when Honey was mentioned. He looked both befuddled and downright fearful.

"Maybe you figured it was Ty. Maybe you figured you didn't want to get your own ass shot off. Maybe you figured if he thought he shot you, he wouldn't keep comin' like a loaded freight train."

Rory seemed to be considering this. Then his face went blank. "You chargin' me with something, Wyatt Earp?"

"Not yet," Pruett said, backing away from the table again. "Zach Canter is driving the gun down to the FBI crime lab in Rock Springs as we speak. We'll have the results back in a day or two. Don't stray far from town."

"Never do."

"Once there was a friend of mine
Who died a thousand deaths
His life was filled with parasites
And countless idle threats."

Neil Young,
Barstool Blues

Chapter 12

SHELLY DELGADO'S body was still in Scoot Alvord's morgue. The bullet the coroner dug from the back of her spine was also a .32 and Pruett sent it to Rock Springs with Rory McIntyre's gun and the other slug.

For the first time in his career, Pruett did not know what to do next. The way this thing was playing out, Rory tried to kill Ty—an act that would have incited any man to consider the option of killing him before a second effort succeeded.

At least in Wind River.

Pruett reached into the lower drawer in his desk and pulled out the bottle of Rebel Yell. He wondered whether Ty had even pulled the trigger. The accused said he only went there to fire off a warning shot or two.

The sheriff downed a mouthful of booze.

None of this meant Ty was innocent of the crime. He pled guilty.

After another guzzle, the razor edges on the questions tumbling in his mind softened some. Cut him less.

He missed Bethy. Needed her back. Either that or he needed something to fill the yearning in his soul. The emptiness would never be assuaged. But the yearning could.

Pruett picked up the phone and dialed.

"Hello?"

"Jesse?"

"Yes, uh, James?"

"It's been a long time, Jess."

"You're drinking again," Jesse Claremont said.

"I'm doing what needs to be done."

"Does 'getting things done' include calling me for the first time in what, ten years?"

"Twelve."

"I'm hanging up, James."

"Wait," Pruett said. "Hear me out."

Silence. Then: "Not here, not on the phone…"

"Let me come over."

It didn't take much talking when he got there. Pruett knew it wouldn't. He did not consider himself a manipulator, but he knew what Jesse Claremont wanted. She'd always wanted him back. And though he loved Bethy with everything he was, Pruett could not deny the instinct inside him that was roused every time he ran into Jesse on the street, or in the store, or at the post office.

He never went back on his promise to Bethy. Not after she took him back. And he knew to do anything now with Jesse would feel like a betrayal—a dishonoring of his memory for his dead wife. But the booze had other ideas. The booze wanted Jesse, and so Pruett wanted her, too.

They didn't embrace but rather fell together. Jesse's sobriety was still intact but Pruett had drunk enough for the two of them.

People want to believe in the good that exists within them. Many do what is expected of them, day upon day, until one of two things happens: they fail or they die young, before they can fail. It's not a pretty truth, but, as imperfect beings, humankind was destined to miss the mark. At least occasionally.

Pruett knew he needed to stop drinking. He knew he never should have given in to the ghosts of his heart. But he *did* give in. And though such reason offered no tangible comfort, the old man decided, for tonight, it would do.

The next morning, Sheriff Pruett rose before the sun and made a quiet exit. The guilt chewed on the frayed edges of his conscience. He needed to talk to someone. His sponsor moved away from Wind River a little more than a year ago. He didn't want to confide in anyone else local. Word moved too fast.

So he waited outside Hanson's hotel room until he saw Wendy leave for her morning run.

"Sheriff Pruett," Hanson said, standing in the door with his robe neatly tied.

"Join me for coffee," Pruett said. "Preferably before my daughter gets back."

"Five minutes."

They drove to the Wrangler. Pruett ordered black coffee. Hanson wanted cream.

"You much of a drinker?" Pruett asked.

"You know I enjoy the occasional whiskey."

"What I mean, you ever had issue with it?"

"I suppose," Hanson said, rubbing day-old whiskers. "Never anything that consumed me."

"Well I've been consumed," Pruett said. "More than a time or two."

"Off the wagon, then."

"Way off. Left the road, the map. Uncharted trails."

"I can't help but expect, with all that's gone on, Sheriff, that such a relapse is more than understandable."

"You remember the woman I told you about?"

"Yes."

"I went to her last night. First time in a dozen years."

"A man needs what he needs, Sheriff. You are alone now. I know that's not how you want to see it, but whether it's been a month, a year, or a lifetime, you are alone."

"Is that supposed to make me feel better?"

"It's supposed to make you feel un-obliged."

"What I feel is guilty."

"Jane Austen said: *Let other pens dwell on guilt and misery.*"

"I figured out that there are different kinds of love. I wasn't always kind to Jesse. It was a different relationship than what I had with…with…"

"Let go of the guilt, Sheriff."

"That it?"

"You need to stop drinking, too."

Pruett stared at the gun. There was only one bullet. The same bullet he'd kept in there since Bethy died. There wasn't anything noble or righteous or symbolic, unless it was representative of the way everything inside him seemed to be quitting.

No one can say for sure what cowardice lurks beneath the veneer of a brave exterior. Not until the first mortar hits; not until the brick fortress of our personal solitude begins to crumble.

If a person is lucky, they find another soul to accompany them on their journey. And if they are blessed, two souls become one. As all clouds are lined with silver, however, so do they all have the potential to grow pregnant with storm. Having a soul mate is indeed a wondrous thing, but when that soul is torn away, the remaining wound of separation can often never heal.

Pruett had jumped headlong down the mountainside, wishing only for a cliff off which to plummet.

Now it was time. Time to decide. Drink another glass and eat a bullet, or cast off his demons and find a way back to himself. Twelve steps had nothing on Sheriff James Pruett's *own* list.

The sheriff picked up the glass of orange whiskey. The aroma climbed to his nostrils like a wily beast, scampering up a twisted vine.

Comfort. The promise of anesthetic for the anguish in his heart.

Numbness at last.

But there was no such truth. No one could simply assuage the pain with a sedative, because you couldn't stay sedated indefinitely.

Unless…

Pruett picked up the revolver. The cool blue metal felt as if it might invade his system. Death seemed a frigid option. The only relief being the return to oblivion.

He laid the pistol on the thick, scarred surface of the worktable. He picked up the bottle, carried it to the utility sink, and poured the liquid evil down the drain.

When he walked from the shed, his courage came with him.

"Who is it?" Beulah Jorgensen asked through the closed office door.

"James Pruett," the sheriff said, opening the door slowly.

She was already waving him off. "We've got nothing to talk about, Sheriff."

"Oh, we do, Ma'am. You just don't understand it yet."

"What the hell is that supposed to mean?"

Pruett sat down and drilled his gaze into her dead eyes. He wanted to hate her for being a part of what killed his girl, but in her face the sheriff saw a sad, lost woman who had sold her integrity for a splash of refreshment.

As sharp as Beulah was in a court of law, this lumbering old maid would never have guessed the terrible machinations her greed could set into motion.

Pruett leaned in. "I know about the payoffs."

Jorgensen choked on her own saliva. "Wh-what? I don't have a notion what you are talking about, Pruett."

"*Sheriff* Pruett. This is official business, Beulah. This is the moment of reckoning. You either talk to me or we take this straight down to Judge Butler, and then you get thrown in the poke."

The Town Attorney said nothing. Silence was her acquiescence.

"Shelly Delgado is in the morgue. Have you taken the time to try and figure the angle on that one?"

"Shelly's murder will be investigated in due time. This office is a little rattled right now, Sheriff."

"She's dead because she helped me dig into your relationship with Rory McIntyre."

"I truly have no idea…"

"Shut up," Pruett snapped. "You listen to what I am saying. I'd like to give you credit for being a smart cookie, Beulah, but I fear you're just another pretender. Built yourself up on the backs of the good folk; clawed and scraped those who did wrong by you all those years ago. But it doesn't make you successful—it only makes you a taker."

"I don't have to listen to this bullshit."

"Yes, Beulah, you *do*. You got my wife killed, you got your own attorney murdered, and you've spent the past month trying to put a noose around Ty McIntyre's neck when you knew all along what set his actions into motion."

"Just what do you think you know, Sheriff Pruett?"

"I know you took the money. I know that you and Rory McIntyre have been fucking each other for years. That a good enough jumping off place for you?"

Beulah Jorgensen looked like she just swallowed a small rodent.

"What I can't figure just yet," Pruett said, "is whether or not you tipped off Rory about Shelly Delgado. You must have, because I can't see anyone else knowing what's what in that regard."

"I was never party to any killing," Beulah said, her bravado all but permanently deflated. "I was never party to any of *that*."

"The ballistics came back. Same gun that was used in the attempt on Ty's life killed Shelly Delgado."

"Jesus."

"Who did you *think* did it, Beulah? How many murders does it take to bring you into the game?"

"Rory's not capable...he's a good man. Hard. But a good man."

"How that old cowpoke is in the sack's got *nothin'* to do with who he is. He's a *scorpion*, Ma'am, and you set him loose on all of us."

"What you see and hear
depends a good deal
on where you are standing;
it also depends on
what sort of person you are."

C.S. LEWIS,
The Magician's Nephew

Perception is too often involuntary,
but hurtful just the same.

PART TWO

Chapter 13

ON THE second morning of the trial, while Ty was away from the jail and Pruett's deputies stood present in court, the sheriff wandered back into the empty cell. There wasn't much to see. A pile of damaged dime store paperbacks. The pro rodeo magazines Wendy had bought her uncle. A shaving kit with a few other sundries. On a whim, Pruett pulled the cot away from the wall. There was a small pile of cement dust and debris on the floor, against the wall. He looked up and saw that Ty had been carving something in the wall. The sheriff leaned in.

Numbers. He was carving numbers into the aged, softening concrete:

7002499

Pruett had no idea what the numbers meant. He was more concerned about what Ty had used to make them. Inside the pillow, pushed through a hole in the fabric and hidden amongst the faux goose down, Pruett found a metal fork with the three tines mashed together into a point and then bent slightly. Ty had made himself a nice little carving tool from a piece of flatware left by an unobservant deputy.

The sheriff made a mental note to give the prisoners only plastic utensils from there on in. He then went back to the empty office and sat down slowly in his chair. Every joint hurt. His back felt like a Slinky that stretched out until someone had tried (unsuccessfully) to push the coils back together, leaving an uneven, unbalanced mess behind. Only when the Slinky was pushed back together it was suddenly made of barbed wire, the points jamming into his spine.

Getting old had not proved to be everything he'd hoped. Actually he never hoped for much. And losing the love of his life had been far harder on him than a bad back, too much girth, drying skin, or any number of other ailments.

He reached into the back of the filing drawer, back past the metal bar where the folders hung, into that secret space. The bottle was there waiting for him. God he used to love a drink while he thought through the facts of the case. Better than buttered popcorn and movies. The warm bite; the way at first it made his mind feel sharper, more tuned into the case.

Pruett slammed the door.

Sharper, yes, until he woke up sleeping on the desk, further behind than when he started because of the splitting headache.

He wrote the numbers down on a pad with a bit of space between them.

7 0 0 2 4 9 9

It sure looked a hell of a lot like a phone number. Wyoming only had one area code—307—and 700 was the prefix to Jackson Hole. Pruett picked up the handset on the phone and punched in the full ten-digit number.

There was only one ring before a female voice answered:

"Bureau of Land Management."

It took only that first day for the prosecution to present its case. Hanson had expected this tactical approach. It was smart. Keep it simple. Keep the jury alert and frosty; don't let them wander off and dream up some other version of the crime. It was for this reason Hanson chose his opening remarks. The prosecution could hardly be accused of being biased if they concentrated primarily on the evidence at hand.

The prosecution called all the people present that night at the ranch—Vance Dustin and the McIntyres who were there: Honey, Rory, and Rance. Jorgensen also marched a few character witnesses through the courtroom who each testified to the violent nature of Ty McIntyre—kept them coming, in fact, until J.W. Hanson objected, stipulating that each of the next dozen or so witnesses would tell a similar story of conflict and/or violence with the accused.

It wasn't as if every member of the jury didn't already know Ty anyway, Hanson argued, which elicited a few chuckles from the box.

Jorgensen did call one final character witness, as Hanson knew she would.

"The prosecution calls Ms. Wendy Steele to the stand."

"Objection," Hanson said, standing up. "Prejudicial and irrelevant."

"The witness testimony is completely relevant. Establishes the defendant's propensity for violence toward *family members*, Your Honor," the prosecutor argued.

"Objection overruled. We've been over this, Mr. Hanson," said Butler. "However, this is a short leash, Ms. Jorgensen. A *very* short leash."

Hanson had filed a motion to exclude Wendy's testimony based solely on the fact that Ty was never convicted of a crime. Butler concurred but felt the testimony from a family member who, according to her own admission on the police report, had been stricken, was appropriate for the jury to hear. The compromise he devised was to allow Jorgensen to question Wendy on whether or not there had been any violence perpetrated against her by the defendant. No mention of charges, a police report, arrest, another trial, or any other details were to be allowed.

Of course, Hanson knew Beulah Jorgensen would do everything in her skillset to get a mention of the charges even to have them stricken from the record. Once in the jury's mind, you didn't strike memories.

"Ms. Steele," the prosecutor said. "You are the daughter of the victim in this case."

"You know I am."

"Your honor, please instruct the witness to answer the question in the affirmative."

"I'll order her to answer the question in a direct manner," Judge Butler said, intentionally allowing a bit of his Wyoming vernacular to slip into the remark. "*How* she answers questions is between her and her oath with God, ma'am."

There was a murmur and cameras hummed and clicked. Butler tried to look judicious.

"Thank you, your honor. Ms. Steele?"

"I don't remember the question."

"I asked if you were the daughter of the victim."

"Then my answer is no."

"Excuse me?"

"You asked me a direct question and I said 'no'. Directly."

"You swore an oath before sitting in that chair, Ms. Steele."

"The victim *is* my mother. Her dying did not change the facts."

Butler shrugged.

"I want this on the record clearly. Are you the daughter of Bethy McIntyre Pruett?"

"No."

"Do you need to be reminded of the penalties for perjury?"

"Her name is Pruett."

"What?"

"She didn't keep her maiden name. Believed rather strongly in it, if I remember correctly. So I won't let you change her name here. For the record, that is. So no, I don't even know anyone by the name you are using."

"Permission to treat the witness as hostile," Jorgensen said.

"Granted."

"Are you her daughter or not?"

"Every person in this courtroom knows I am."

"At your parent's home on Green Ridge when you were but fifteen years old, did the accused, Mr. Tyree McIntyre strike you across the face with his fist, breaking your orbital socket?"

"No," Wendy said.

"I'll remind you *again* of your sworn oath, Ms. Steele."

"It was fractured, not broken. You should get your facts straight."

"And were you indeed fifteen at the time of your orbital socket being fractured by the defendant's fist?"

"I don't recall."

"You were fifteen," Jorgensen said.

"Is that a question?"

Judge Butler looked sternly at Wendy. "The witness will answer."

"Yes, I was fifteen."

"So you admit that the defendant is capable of perpetrating violence against his own family. A young girl—a child?"

"I most certainly do not."

"But you said…"

"I told you what happened. That's what you asked me."

"And being stricken does not equate to an act of violence?"

"Violence is wanton, ma'am. I was stricken *accidentally*."

"That is not an answer to the question I asked. Your honor, this is going nowhere," said Jorgensen.

"I am inclined to agree, Madam Prosecutor. I believe you've established what you set out to establish."

"With due respect, how is it you know what I am after?"

"I do know. And you're done here. Approach."

Hanson and Jorgensen walked forward to the bench. Butler covered his microphone.

"This has been discussed at length," the judge hissed. "The defendant was never convicted of anything. All parties say the same thing, including the police report. You've been allowed to introduce the act by deposing Ms. Steele. She admitted to being struck by the defendant. Accidentally, I might add."

"Then I ask you to strike the word 'accidentally' from the record."

"Request denied," said Butler.

"She's not answered one of my questions directly, Your Honor."

"On the contrary, ma'am. She has answered each of your questions directly. That you are unable to engage a tripwire and force the witness to say something disallowable by this courtroom so that the jury might hear it even *after* I ruled such testimony prejudicial to the accused is your own failure, not hers. Move away."

To the courtroom, Butler said: "Your witness for cross, Mr. Hanson."

"No questions, Your Honor," Hanson said, and flashed the jury a slight smirk.

The call came on Pruett's cell phone later that night, when he was home, busy washing a week's worth of dishes caked with the grime of unwanted bachelorhood.

"Pruett," the sheriff said.

"That murderer's going to fry, Sheriff. Thought you'd want to know." The voice was muffled, as if the words were spoken through gelatin.

"Who the hell is calling?" Pruett said.

"An interested citizen. The jurors, we know where the bear shits, sir."

"So you're on the jury. Calling the county sheriff. Not smart. Not smart at all."

"I figured you'd be happy," the caller said. "Figured I was callin' the widower of a murdered wife 'stead of some dumb…"

"Dumb *what?*" Pruett growled.

The call disconnected. Pruett wondered about how much stock to put in such a call. Number one, even if it were true, it was no big surprise. Hanson was losing the case. It wasn't like it had the gleam of a winner in the first place. And he couldn't prove it was a juror. And he sure as hell didn't have a clue as to which one, anyway—though because of the near commentary, he had a couple ideas.

Pruett didn't know how to feel about the call, either. Assuming the information was accurate. He'd tried to be impartial about the trial, the outcome and verdict—and Ty had, after all, let him live. He'd also stayed put to face the music; he could have headed off for Canada with the sheriff alive or dead and he didn't. The old sheriff wasn't sure if those facts alone made the defendant worthy of admiration. More than a small part of him had wanted to die up in the wilderness. Die or kill his wife's murderer—or both—and there still wasn't any reconciliation on either of those counts.

Besides, he was on the side of the law. People guilty of murder were supposed to be found guilty. And as far as Pruett knew it, Ty McIntyre was guilty. He may not have intended to kill her—hell, he might not have intended to kill *anyone*—but he'd shot Bethy. There was no disputing that.

Or was there?

Something about the whole situation seemed off. And that something had been worming its way into Pruett's brain since the very start. The sheriff grabbed his hunting coat and his hat. He had some questions of his own he wanted to ask and he wasn't going to wait until the attorneys got around to asking them.

"Wake up, Ty."

Ty rolled over and look up at the cage door. "Weren't asleep."

"I brought us coffee," said Pruett.

Ty stood and rolled his neck, joints snapping like tiny kernels of popcorn going off in his spine. "Gettin' old's hell, Sheriff. And that cot you all tryin' to pass of as a bed ain't helpin' matters none."

Pruett handed a lidded cup of black coffee through the bars. "They didn't have any cream," he said.

"Don't take none. Obliged for the hot joe."

"I want to talk to you, man to man," Pruett said, pulling a chair over and sitting his two hundred and forty pounds down in it.

"Always do," Ty said.

"Another one of those 'off the record' kinda deals," the sheriff said.

"Hmm. Not sure that's a grand idea anymore. With the trial and all."

"Why do you want to die so bad?" Pruett said.

"Each of us owes a death," Ty said. "Some of us owe a pile more'n one."

"You told me once that you didn't remember shooting that night."

"I remember enough," Ty said.

"Tell me again."

"I remember tearin' over there like a banshee, nearly tippin' over the truck twice on that piece a shit road…then…hmm…stopped before I got there. I got out the truck and set my ass down on a big rock. Wanted to think."

"What about?" Pruett said.

"All of it. How my old man could try and kill me. His son."

"Didn't sit well."

"No it did *not*. But I got to thinkin'. Past the anger touched off in my skull…methodical kind of thoughts."

"Like what?"

"Like how killin' Rory weren't just about me, or about revenge. It would be like wipin' a scourge from the Earth."

"Meaning?"

"He's no good, Sheriff. Everyone's bad, in one way or another. But Rory's kind…they just go on hurtin' and hurtin'. Never fuckin' stops. I drove over thinkin' I would be the one to put an end to it."

"But your conscience got the better of you."

"You serious?" Ty said.

"Let's say thinking about doing it and doing it are *not* one and the same," Pruett said.

"That's goddamned right."

"I knew when you asked me if I killed anyone in 'Nam," Pruett said. "Knew you couldn't have done it."

"How so?"

"You had a look in your eyes," the sheriff said.

"What look?"

"There's this look a man gets in his eye when he talks about taking another life. It's a look of awe. Like the act itself is this sacred thing, which it damn sure is. Once a man has killed, though, he loses that look."

"That's why I stopped and started drinkin' some more," Ty said.

"I know. Didn't help, did it?" Pruett said.

"No."

"Nothing can help that, Ty. Nothing."

"I decided then and there I was going to warn 'em, though. Just put the fear of the devil in their hearts."

"You think about winging one of them?"

"Sure. Considered pickin' a few a them gray hairs off the old man's head."

"You're a helluva shot," Pruett said. "Just the kind who could do it."

"'Cept I had a few more drinks."

"Passed out, did you?"

"Yep. Sat down on my rear end and fell over. Went directly to sleep. Everything else was a blackout."

"Why haven't you told all this to your attorney?"

"I have told him. Why you think he's arguin' I didn't intend to kill no one?"

"I mean the part about you passing out."

"I did. Told everyone I blacked out."

"You just said you passed out. Took a nap, as it were."

"No difference," Ty said.

"Yeah, well I say there is," the sheriff said, standing up, pushing the chair back across the stone floor.

"What's that?"

"All the times I ever got drunk," Pruett said. "All those times I blacked out, you know I never once actually remember passing out? That's why they call it a blackout. You don't remember anything."

"I don't follow."

"Man passing out, Ty, just ain't the same thing as him *blacking out*."

"You've lost your mind," Ty said. "Black out, pass out. Damn you if you think there's a difference."

"You didn't shoot anyone, did you, Ty?"

"Fuck you, Pruett."

"Your truck was there. *You* were there. But you didn't pull that trigger, did you?"

"I said *fuck you*, sir."

"Who're you protecting, Ty? Who's worth one of those deaths owed?"

"We're done talking."

Pruett walked away and never said a word about the phone number his prisoner had carved in the wall. He also neglected to mention the homemade etcher, made of a fork—the one that Pruett had returned to its hiding place wondering just what his wife's accused murderer might carve next.

Pruett left the jail with nothing but drinking and sleeping on his mind.

The sheriff bought a bottle of Heaven Hill on his way home. All that talk of drinking with Ty had done him in. He thought about what little weakness it took for a man to acquiesce to his sworn addiction. He could spend *years* walking away from that goddamned bottle and yet the first sip was always just 'round the next bend. Pruett had bounced on and off the wagon before; all drunks ever needed was an excuse, and never a grand one either. Before his twelve years of sobriety Pruett had quit and restarted a hundred times. He'd started drinking because his back hurt him or because a particular day on the job was worse than another. He justified drinking when it was too damned cold out, and then he reached for a bottle of something when it was too fucking *hot*.

No sir, I only drink under two conditions: when I'm alone or when I'm with somebody.

There was always an excuse. The reason, however, remained the same.

Fill the hole.

Every man had one. Some had a hundred. Hell, when God brought souls up to Heaven, Pruett guessed some fellas' souls probably looked like they'd been carved up with a Thompson gun. But Pruett had long since figured the secret:

It didn't matter how *many*. All that mattered was THE hole. And there was always one. For the habitual drunk, it was simply easier to find.

Negative space. The abyss of a soul.

And as life rolled on, the abyss, it only got bigger.

Now, after the death of his sweet Bethy, Pruett felt like the emptiness inside him knew no boundaries—as if all the other holes in him had finally caved into the One. Endless, like a canyon at night. Or a well in which you never heard the rock hit bottom.

He spun the cap off his new bottle with one thick thumb and then he drank.

He relished the heat as it ran through him. It was like a thousand tiny fires burning in his heart and in his belly.

He knew the void he was pouring the booze into would never be filled.

But he figured maybe he could burn it out. Let the damn thing consume the whole of him.

How then would he know the pain, when there was nothing left with which to compare it?

He sipped on the bourbon and reread the copy of the will. There was nothing out of the ordinary. Hanson said it himself: it was stock issue, pure boilerplate. The land was divided equally.

And yet it was *not*.

Dirk never wanted anything to do with the ranch. So Willy never gave him any land.

Dirk, however, likely would have known nothing about the mineral rights. Not until Ty told him, anyway. Or he heard it shouted in one of the bars.

So why had Dirk been squawking all these months? Money-wise, he was taking it in the shorts as much as Ty.

And where *was* Dirk? He'd not shown up at trial. The other boys and the old man, they never came either, except when they were called to the stand of course. But they were ranchers—their sustenance depended on daylight hours; they couldn't be troubled to get splinters in their ass on the courtroom benches.

Dirk could have come. Out of pure curiosity he should have come.

Pruett picked up the phone and called for the number to the Flying Q Guest Ranch.

"Flyin' Q," a throaty woman answered.

"This Marigold?" Pruett said.

"Depends who's on the other end a this line."

"Sheriff James Pruett."

"Well, Hell's bells, Sheriff. Why'd you not say so?"

"I need to speak to Dirk McIntyre. Is he on the trail?"

"Dirk's not on any trail that I know of," Marigold Potter said. "He's been off sick for more'n a week."

"Sick?"

"He called in last Monday. Sounded turrible. Couldn't hardly tell it was him."

"You haven't talked to him since?"

"Nope."

"All right then, thanks a heap, Mari."

"Sure thing. Sheriff, I never made it to Bethy's service. I'm sure sorry for your loss."

"Thanks," said Pruett and hung up the phone before the hole in him grew any bigger.

He had to sober up first, so Pruett brewed himself a pot of campfire coffee—threw the grounds right in the kettle on the stove, boiled it up, and poured it into his favorite mug. He drank the swill as fast as he could. Then he went upstairs and turned on a cold shower.

Pullin' every cliché out of the book for this one, he thought.

He needed to get over to Dirk's place.

After three cups of the strong coffee, a long, frigid shower, and an hour of walking around the property, fiddling with this and that—anything to keep the blood flowing and the mind busy—Pruett had sobered up pretty well.

He grabbed the keys to the county Suburban and drove toward the northeast of town and Green River Mesa Road, where Dirk McIntyre owned a small piece of property that backed up to Pine Creek.

The driveway down into the front yard had been swallowed up by willow branches over the years and they whipped the side of Pruett's truck as he wobbled down the half-washed-out road onto the property.

Dirk's yellow and white Chevy pickup was parked out front. The yard was scattered with junk—an old, rusted riding lawnmower that looked as if it hadn't been ridden in a dozen summers; at least two cases' worth of empty Pabst Blue Ribbon cans; also every kind of tire known to mankind.

The shades were pulled and the front door locked. Pruett knocked. Several times. Banged on the door with the heel of his hand, even. There was no answer.

Pruett went around back. He could hardly hear himself think with the creek roaring by just ten or twenty yards away. The back door was locked, too. Pruett thought of Shelly Delgado, lying dead twelve hours in the sticky slop of her own blood.

Shelly Delgado hadn't been a suspect in his wife's murder, though. If Pruett broke in and found something useful, it wouldn't be admissible. Even in the tiny town of Wind River, Wyoming, the days of kangaroo courts and vigilante justice were long gone. The county sheriff couldn't kick down a door any more legally than the next man or woman.

Pruett walked down toward Pine Creek, thinking maybe he could find a branch and put it through the window in Dirk's back door. There had been some hellacious windstorms the night before. If Dirk was not home, or even if he was sleeping the sleep of the inebriated, Pruett could leave the branch and no one would be the wiser. If he found something he'd just have to figure a way to get a search warrant. Pruett couldn't afford to leave now and wait. Things were moving too fast.

Rummaging through the willow branches near the water's edge, he saw the cowboy boot sticking partway out of the water. Pruett knelt down and then saw the frayed end of a pair of jeans and the white, fish-colored leg inside one. Nine tenths of the body was submerged. It looked as if someone had tied off the body like a string of fish—staked the heavy chain real deep in the ground, secured it around the leg, and then just let the current keep the line taut and the body submerged by whitewater. The icy river would stave off decomposition and the smell that went with it for weeks, maybe even months. In fact, Pruett guessed, the flesh would wash off the leg and release the body first—someone would find the corpse long before anyone smelled it.

Clearly Rory, Rance, or Cort—or some combination of those greedy players—had killed Dirk.

Occam's razor.

Simplest theory first.

Pruett pulled his cell phone and called his team.

*"Billy Mack
is a detective down in Texas.
You know he knows just exactly
what the facts is.
He ain't gonna let those two
escape justice.
He makes his livin' off of the
people's taxes."*

Steve Miller Band,
Take the Money and Run

R.S. GUTHRIE

Chapter 14

THE BODY they fished out of the river was Dirk McIntyre's. He had suffered mightily before the killer—or killers—finished him off. There were lacerations crisscrossing the ex-cowpoke's wide, muscular back as if he'd been whipped over and again.

"Someone was trying awful hard to get information out of that boy," Pruett said. He had invited J.W. Hanson to meet him at the Wooden Boot.

"And you think you know what information that is?" said Hanson.

"Not exactly. But I have an idea where to start."

"Ty didn't react at all to the news. My client has piss in his veins."

"Not surprising," the sheriff said. "You've known him a few weeks. No one in this town would be hoping for a Hallmark moment with Ty McIntyre."

"Fair enough."

"My guess? Ty's been punishing himself enough on the inside. More than we can know."

"And if you believe in Heaven and Hell, then there just might be a further reckoning," J.W. Hanson said.

Sheriff Pruett sipped on his bourbon while Waylon Jennings warbled from the dilapidated jukebox at the Wooden Boot's door. "As a matter of fact, I don't believe in 'em. I think all the reckoning we get is right here in front of us, every day."

"I thought you quit the drink," Hanson said.

"I did. Then I started it again."

"Never begrudge a man the pleasures of the flesh."

"You sure are a mouthy one."

"It's the lawyer in me. You know what a pack of shitbags we are."

"That I do."

Hanson smiled and called for another round. "My client tells me you came to see him—that it was *you* that wanted to tell him personally about Dirk."

"What I wanted," Pruett said, "is for him to come clean now that his accomplice is dead."

"Like I said, he's not talking. Not even to me."

"I asked you here for a favor," Pruett said.

"Let's hear it."

"I want you to ask my daughter to speak with him."

Hanson sipped his own drink, weighing the request. "Why wouldn't you ask her yourself?"

"Our relationship just started back on the mend. I don't want her thinking I'm interfering."

"But asking me to do it, that doesn't qualify?"

"Not if she doesn't know I asked."

"Message received. And I'll say yes, but for one reason only: it is in the best interest of my client to tell the whole story. If you think Wendy can convince him, then it's worth a try."

"Thanks," Pruett said as the new drinks arrived. "Put this round on me."

Deputy Baptiste walked Wendy back to the jail.

"Been a while since I seen you around here," Baptiste said.

"I've sort of kept away."

"My family is still on the reservation. All but a brother, and he died. I don't visit home all that much."

"Some of your family worked on our property once."

"Many, many years ago."

"I don't remember them," Wendy said. "My father told me."

"We're even then. I don't remember 'em either."

Wendy's uncle was sitting up on the tussled blanket of the cot, reading a Louis L'Amour paperback, an author who he stated on several occasions he did not cater to. Sheriff Pruett kept an old stack of them for the prisoners.

"Hi, Uncle Ty."

"Darlin'," Ty said and stood slowly, rubbing his corded back muscles. "Sorry for the mess. The accommodations leave a bundle to be desired."

He met her at the bars and put his arms out to hug her. "Not exactly tickled for you to see me like this," he said.

"I've seen you like this before."

"Yeah. Growin' up all those years, your father bein' sheriff, I guess you have. Damn good to see you, girl. I owe ya a debt of thanks for findin' me a lawyer, too."

"You don't owe me anything. He's really good. And..."

"You don't have to say more, young 'un. I knowed the first time he talked about you that the two of you was in love."

"What makes you think *that*," Wendy said, red flushing her cheekbones as a balloon fills with air.

"Fellas git this funny look on their face when they talk about their own gal. I seen it on the professor. More'n once."

"I'm not sure it's love," Wendy said.

"Don't matter."

"So you know, he took the case because he wants to help you; because he believes in you."

"Don't matter neither."

"I'm sorry about Dirk," Wendy said.

"Me, too. We weren't brothers much anymore—wasn't no secret how I felt about him. But that don't mean I appreciate it when family turns on its own."

"Did someone turn on him?"

"Clearly."

"Family, I mean."

"Don't have a say on that," Ty said.

"I came here because I think it's important that you tell your attorney what really happened that night when Mom died."

"Then you wasted a trip, baby girl. I've said all I'm gonna."

"Sheriff Pruett will be going after the people that killed Dirk. You could help him by giving him the whole truth, Uncle Ty."

"Dirk got his own self killed."

"Did Pruett tell you what the killers did to him?" Wendy said.

"Found him in the river, the sheriff said. Guessin' he drowned."

"It was worse than that. Whoever killed him was looking for answers."

"What did they do?"

Wendy told Ty what his brother's body looked like when it was pulled from the river. She shared with him the gruesome specifics of Scoot's autopsy. Ty sat back on his cot, drained of all tenaciousness.

"They whipped him," Ty said. "Like a fucking *animal* those bastards *whipped him*."

Wendy nodded solemnly.

"I guess there's a reckoning due."

"Was it Rory?" Wendy said.

"Weren't Rory," Ty said. "It was mother. Whatever those bastards did to Dirk, Honey McIntyre ordered it done."

"I'm a child, I'm a mother
I'm a sinner, I'm a saint
I do not feel ashamed
I'm your hell, I'm your dream
I'm nothing in between"
Meredith Brooks, *Bitch*

Chapter 15

PRUETT SAT in thundering silence. They'd known Ty was protecting someone. In his mind the sheriff could see Honey holding Bethy in her lap, stroking her hair as she had a hundred times before. Her baby. Her little girl.

"Why would he say that?" Hanson said.

"Because he meant it," said Wendy. "What I mean is, he'd never make up something like that."

Pruett still said nothing. Even if Honey McIntyre was conspiring whatever was happening in his town, she wasn't the murderer. There was no way she held the whip.

"Is Ty ready to talk about who did the killing?" Pruett finally said.

"He said he would only talk to you," Wendy told him.

"Only to me..."

"Says he owes it to you."

"I need to talk to you first, Wendy," Pruett said.

"You've never called me that."

"It's your name, ain't it? Can we walk to the park?" Pruett said.

"Let's go."

Pruett and his daughter sat on the bench; the same bench where he'd sat not long ago and held her close to him, remembering when she was a little baby, how perfect he believed their love would always be.

"Things are getting dangerous around here," he said. "I've never been afraid of my duty, or shirked it, and I never will, but I *do* fear there are things going on that we hadn't thought of; things that might be more than a small county sheriff's department can handle."

"Things you can share with me?" Wendy said.

"Things I'd rather not. For your own safety."

"I get it," she said, and put her hand in his.

"Before this goes any further—before anything happens—I wanted to have this talk with you," the sheriff said. "And I want to do it sober. You deserve *at least* that much from me."

"I don't like the way you're talking."

"I don't like what's happening in this town. I know who I *can* rely on. Problem is, I am not exactly sure who I *can't*."

"I'm not sure I understand."

Pruett looked skyward. He was avoiding what he really wanted to say to her.

"Things are going to get worse around here," he said. "Not what you'd call normal small town worse. If anything should happen, there're things we've still left unsaid."

"Sheriff…"

"Wendy, I know why you hated me all those years."

"I never hated you."

"Fair enough. Then I know why you stayed away."

"I don't think you do," she said. "I'm not sure I know those answers anymore. You know how things build up inside a person? It gets to the point where you can't blame only one side or the other. The silence—not giving you a chance to know what I was feeling inside. I played my part."

Pruett squeezed her hand tighter. "For a long time I thought the deck was so stacked against us we'd never find solid ground again," he said. "Vietnam, that damned medal I didn't deserve, the affair. And the election…"

Wendy looked up into his eyes.

"Yeah, girl, I know. At least I know now. Back then, I guess I looked at it in a different way. As if I could pretend I was something—some*one*—different than who I was."

"That's just it," Wendy said. "There is nothing about you—least of all the color of your skin—that makes you less a man than anyone in this town."

"I never felt less of a man. Never. Growing up black in a town like Wind River, well, there are going to be challenges. And you figure out that you deal with those challenges by either fighting them every chance you get or by not giving them any heed. I just chose to make it go away by ignoring it—by letting the people of this town voice their acknowledgement of me as a man—not a man of color, but as *their sheriff*—by the vote."

"I know that now," she said softly.

Pruett turned to her but he was looking at a place far from where they sat. "I know you needed me to defend myself. And not just you. Bethy. My lineage. Not just for what it meant to me, Sheriff James Pruett. I know now that was selfish."

"You want to hear something that will surprise you?" Wendy said. Pruett nodded his head.

"It was the first time in my life that I ever felt we were different."

Pruett was reelected his first three additional terms. In fact, he was unopposed in all but the first election, when he won his Sheriff's badge. In the fourth reelection, however, a rancher named Percy Villines announced his candidacy.

The campaign, it got heated. And dirty.

James Pruett knew his family—young and old—went against everything most small western towns considered "normal". But there, in his town—his *ancestors'* town—he'd never really felt out of place. There were times. Times when families like the McIntyres, in fact, made it known in somewhat covert terms that they didn't ever really accept, deep down, that a black family could be pioneers and landowners in a western town.

But the Pruetts had been in Wind River before it even had a name. When it was nothing but prairies, mountains, and people with the courage and determination to stay alive. They'd stuck it out. Made a life for themselves just like any other family.

And generations later, when James Pruett—only a child—fell in love with Bethy McIntyre, even one of the meanest, most racist families in the township could not stop them from being together.

That wasn't enough for James Pruett, though. He had wanted to prove to the McIntyres and to any other family that harbored secret, deep-rooted, unacceptable beliefs that a black man *could* be elected sheriff in a Wyoming town, that they were wrong.

And he had won his first election by a landslide. Wind River loved James Pruett and it had nothing to do with the color of his skin. Even the McIntyres had eventually accepted his presence in their lives, if only for the merit of his heart and the quality of man he was.

Then, in the fourth term of Sheriff James Pruett's office, Percy Villines took it upon himself to try and rally those old school men and women in the county—families like the McIntyres, and the Holcombs, and at least a few others.

Villines called out Pruett's record, which he defended.

The candidate said it was time for a change, and Pruett told the town it wasn't; told them he'd serve them as he had *always* served them.

Percy Villines then used his platform to get people to speak up. He said a black man had no place being the Sheriff of Sublette County; that the good people of Wind River could not place their *trust* in a man like James Pruett. Villines said the fact that the Pruett family was even allowed to stake claim to land in the territory had always been an injustice, and a permanent blight on their community. He commented, too, on Pruett's mixed marriage, making deep innuendos that the sheriff's family was a disgrace and Villines was taking it upon himself to be the one to say so; the one to try and make things right.

James Pruett refused to comment on the accusations. In truth, he never had to. The residents of the county spoke their minds in the vote. Never before had any elected official in the state (or maybe anywhere else in the country) won an election by the margin Sheriff James Pruett defeated Percy Villines. The challenger received exactly three votes. Presumably himself, his wife, and his eldest son. Whether the McIntyres or the Holcombs ever voted would never be known, but they did not vote *against* Pruett, and that made a statement, too.

A week after the election—after more than a few death threats—the Villines ranch house and every building on the property were burned to the ground while the family watched in horror. They left town the next morning and Pruett went on being sheriff. The debris of the Villines ranch was cleared away, the land auctioned to the highest bidder.

"Baby," Pruett said, holding his daughter tight in his grip. "I never meant to hurt you. I always believed the burden was mine. My ancestors. But I know now I let you and your mother down. I refused to lower myself, to even acknowledge that there was anything to talk about when it came to such accusations. But I owed it to you and Bethy to defend what was *ours*. I needed to defend our *family*; I needed to defend you, dear girl."

Wendy continued to cry.

Pruett held her, his own eyes swelled and tired. So tired. "I didn't defend our honor. And for that, I will never forgive myself. I never have," he said.

Wendy pulled away. She stared him in the eyes.

"*You* were the one who was right. I'm the one who needs forgiveness. And I'll never get it, not from my mother, maybe not from you..."

"I think we forgave each other, don't you?" Pruett said, and smiled wide for the first time since Bethy died. "We've got each other now. And your mother forgave you the moment you walked out the door. It was me kept the feud alive. My pride kept us apart."

"The same God-awful pride I inherited from you," Wendy said, and laughed softly.

The two of them held each other again, and the warmth that enveloped Pruett made him wonder if God really had forgiven him his sins.

Ty faced Pruett down through the bars of his cell. Pruett thought back to the night he'd tried to kill the prisoner. What if he had succeeded? It just proved to him that things were never, ever what they seemed.

"Bethy never said a thing. Not in forty plus years," he said to Ty.

"Ma wouldn't have any of us talkin' about family dealins."

"I always thought Bethy's problems were with the old man—with Rory."

"Rory couldn't shit without permission from his old lady," Ty said lowly.

It hurt Pruett—hurt him deeply—that Bethy had not entrusted him with this secret. "Bethy said she went out there that night because Rory asked her to. She told me he wanted to make amends, have a family night again."

"If Rory asked her it was because Honey said so."

"How did things get so twisted up, Ty?"

"I take it that Delgado lady didn't show you the balance sheets."

"She never got the chance."

"Twenty million dollars enough to twist things up for you?"

"Jesus."

"The gas company found a pocket underneath the main ranch bigger'n the whole patch they're drillin' out west."

"You ready to talk about what happened that night?"

"I figure to tell you the whole thing."

"Then start talking."

"Before I forget, you gotta get ahold a that *lockbox*," Ty said.

"What lockbox?"

Dirk McIntyre scanned the bar for his brother. He found him at a thick, scarred pine table far in the back, half-hidden by shadow.

"Thanks for comin'," Dirk said as he sat down.

"Was comin' here regardless. You know that," Ty said.

"Just the same," Dirk said throwing his head back at Pearly Jo Milton, who was waiting tables. "A Bud," he told her.

"What the fuck you want, Dirk?"

Ty was antsy. Full of fight. It was just one of those nights and all he wanted was to tie on a big one and kick the shit out of someone.

"Been talkin' to some folks," Dirk said. "Specifically, a lady at the courthouse. She don't want her name getting' out. But she wanted me to see some information on our property situation."

"What property situation?" Ty said. "And for your information, you incredible dipshit, everyone in three counties knows you've been diddlin' Juanita Pike for over a year. You know, the *Juanita Pike* who happens to work at the *courthouse*."

"Everyone knows that?"

"Good God, brother, I never even *listen* to gossip, so if I know it…"

"Shit," said Dirk. "Anyway, you're gonna want to see what she gave me."

"Hand it over," Ty said and threw back a shot of Wild Turkey. The whiskey burned in his gut. A few more and he'd go and knock someone off a barstool. Maybe two.

"You promise Juanita's name never gets in this thing."

"Let me see it," Ty snarled, waving for another shot. "Make it a double and make it two of 'em."

Dirk handed his brother the document, a copy of their grandfather's will.

"Lawyer mumbo jumbo," Ty said. Pearly Jo set down two double Turkeys and Ty threw the first one back without even taking his eyes off his brother.

"Look at page seventeen," Dirk said. "Some fair-weather provision or whatnot."

"Fairness provision," Ty mumbled. "Least I can fuckin' *read* when I'm drunk."

"I ain't drunk. And yeah, that's it. Says the minerals are for *all* of us, Ty. *All of us*, not just Pa and the others. Even me, and I ain't got any land at all," Dirk said.

"Even you..."

"Grandpa wanted us all to have a share, if money ever came the family's way, I mean. What're you thinkin', Ty?"

"I'm thinkin' no money came our way, now did it? I'm also thinkin' family just don't do *family* like this." He swallowed the second double in one smooth motion, his eyes red like volcano fire. "Who else knows about this?"

"Juanita said Beulah Jorgensen. Because her name is on the document. And because nothin' happens in this town without that bitch knowin' somethin' about it."

"Beulah."

"I think we should kill 'em," Dirk said. "Keep all the money for ourselves."

"Can't say I disagree," said Ty. "But we gotta be smart about this."

The two sat in silence, ordered more booze, and still said nothing for ten or fifteen minutes. Dirk was waiting on Ty. Ty was getting his drunk on.

He always thought better when he was drunk. Always fought better, too, but he knew he needed to go and get those papers—the original will and some BLM paperwork and maps—secured in his lockbox.

The next night the two of them met at Dirk's place on the river. Ty told Pruett *that's* when they formed a plan to take out the old man. Both of them knew that their mother was behind the whole swindle—that their father wouldn't make any kind of move without her telling him to do it. But Dirk said killing the old man would send her a message. And at least they'd get their share then.

Later that night, at his own home, is when a bullet meant for Ty's skull ended up in the plaster and dry wall of his living room instead of his brain. After the murderer fled, Ty got in his truck and tried to give chase. When he lost the taillights, he headed back to town; back to Dirk's place.

"Wake up," Ty yelled as he pounded on Dirk's door.

Dirk opened the door and Ty barreled through.

"Fucker tried to *kill* me."

"Who? When?"

"Our sweet old pappy. Tried to put a slug 'n my head not one hour ago."

"Shit."

"Damn right *shit*. Who else did that bitch tell?"

"What bitch?"

"Juanita, God DAMN it, don't fuck around with me, boy."

"Shit, Ty...I don't think she told anyone."

"You don't think. Since when anyone told you to *think*?"

"She's good friends with the Drake woman."

"*Maisy* Drake?"

"Yep."

"Maisy Drake's husband drinks pitchers every other night with Rance," Ty said. He was seething. Juanita tells Maisy, Maisy tells her dipshit husband, husband spills the beans to their brother, Rance. It all made sense. Then it took his mother all of twenty-four hours to decide to have Ty killed instead.

Her own son.

"Why the fuck didn't they come after you?" Ty said.

"W-what?"

"I said, they tried to *kill me*. How'd *you* get off scot-free?"

"Maybe you scare them more than I do."

"Maybe."

"Shit, Ty. Wasn't me. I didn't say nothin'. Not to no one. Not by a long shot."

"Tomorrow night, then," Ty said. "We finish it. Once Rory's dead, they'll all start singin' a different song. Even ma. She'll see she was right to fear me."

"So you both went there with murder on your minds?" Pruett said.

"Yep. But halfway there I got them willies we talked about."

"And Dirk was all right with that?"

"Seemed to be. We got more liquored up by that rock, the one I said. I told him I was too drunk to shoot. He wanted to do it."

"You couldn't see who was on the porch," Pruett said.

"Just that fucking *hat*. And the coat. From a distance, it looked like Rory had stepped onto the porch."

"Dirk fired the shot."

"He was too drunk to be firin' any weapon," Ty said, sorrow in his voice. "I shouldn't a let him take that potshot."

"You think Dirk told your old man about the plan, thinkin' he could get a bigger piece of the pie with you out of the picture?"

"I think he told *Honey*."

Pruett thought about that for a moment. "I think he told the BLM."

Ty said nothing, but he flinched.

"You said you were going to tell me all of it," Pruett told him. "*Tell it*."

"I don't know all of it," Ty said as softly as Pruett had ever heard him speak. "That's why I left that number for you to find. I knew the government was involved somehow. Dirk knew more. A lot fuckin' more. That night in the bar, outta the blue he starts flappin' his gums about this huge scam with the government, and how ma and pa was flat smack in the middle of it."

"So how did the shooting go down?"

"Just like I said it did. I figured all that talk was bullshit. The night Bethy died, that happened just like I said. 'Cept…"

"'Cept *what*?"

"Dirk had this cagey look on his face when we tore hell for the south entrance. All the way out to the highway, where we left his pickup. Like he was nervous 'bout somethin'."

"What do you mean?"

"I mean he looked like the cat that ate the fucking canary. Like he was screwin' up the courage for somethin' but just couldn't do it. Like he was too scared to follow through."

"You think you know what that something was?"

"I think he was meant to plunk one in me when we got back to the highway and he yellowed up."

"That means the shooting up at the ranch wasn't any accident."

Pruett decided it was time to pay a visit to Honey McIntyre. If she was at the head of the family, that meant she was the one dealing with the BLM. And Pruett needed to start putting the pieces together fast, or things were going to spiral out of his control.

On the way down the cratered road to the ranch, the cornered animal returned to his gut. The aching need for a drink gnawed at his insides, tormenting him. He didn't want to have this conversation. Hell, it didn't even sound *rational*. But he was past not believing these things could happen in his town. Past thinking such notions were crazy. Too many people were dead or dying to not believe it was true:

Honey McIntyre, crime matriarch.

It was no longer as ridiculous as it once seemed.

And there was certainly nothing ridiculous about Ty's eyes when he talked about his mother. Tyree McIntyre was a powder keg full of fury and a brawler that no man should want to mess with—Pruett himself could now attest to the truth in that statement. But when Ty talked about Honey, the rawness in his voice dissipated and his countenance got all screwed up with, well, *fear*. And Pruett had never seen Ty afraid of anything; the man faced down seething bulls for fun.

But he was damn sure wary of his own mother. That much was evident in the way he deferred to her, even in his speech.

Pruett had intentionally shown up in the middle of the day. Nine times out of ten Rory and anyone else working that day would be out to the upper place. Which would leave him alone to question Honey McIntyre.

God he wanted a drink.

He knocked on the kitchen door. He could see Honey fretting with some baked goods, apron on just so, having to be careful picking up the pans and bowls because of her severe arthritis.

"James A. Pruett," she said warmly when she turned around and saw it was him. "Come in, come in. I just put a new pot of coffee on—be ready in a couple minutes."

Pruett removed his hat and played with his hair some. He walked into the kitchen.

"Sit," Honey said, smiling gently, clearly unperturbed by his presence.

She continued to flit around the kitchen, putting what smelled to be two loaves of pumpkin bread on a cooling rack on one counter then moving the used dishes to the sink for cleaning. "I might ask you to help with these dishes before you leave," she said. "The affliction is mighty hard to take today."

Honey always called her arthritis "the affliction". Ever since Pruett had known her. Until today he'd found it endearing.

"Honey, I…"

She stifled him with a hand in the air. "Coffee first. Civilized people don't have conversation without a cup. Not serious conversation, anyway."

She shuffled over to the cupboard and retrieved two clean, white porcelain cups. "Coffee makers now got a stop-plug, lets the impatient cusses git their coffee 'afore it's done. What'll they think of next to make our lives less troublesome?"

"Don't know," Pruett said.

"Damn tongue a yours is usually flappin' this way and that," Honey said as she sat down and pushed a cup of coal black coffee halfway between them. "Sounds like you got a piece a tanner's leather in there today."

Pruett slid the cup the rest of the way and picked it up for a sip. "Thanks for the coffee," he said.

"You here officially, James?"

"I am."

"Figured as much. Ty's weak. Always has been." Honey sipped at her steaming coffee and then stopped. "I'm of course doing us both the courtesy of assuming that son of mine has gotten to talking about family matters."

"You could say that."

"I'm going to respect *you* enough, James, not to waste your time acting like I don't know what he's told you."

"I just need to get to the bottom of all this mess," Pruett said. "Bethy was your daughter. I'd hope you want the same thing."

"Bethy was my daughter, that's true enough," Honey said. "You further delving into McIntyre matters won't dig her up out of the ground though, now will it?"

"*Excuse me?*"

"She's dead, James. Be a man about it. We took you into the family, even against better judgment."

"I'm not sure I know what you're driving at, Honey, but I can tell you it ain't settling very good in my stomach."

"I'm sorry," she said, taking another small sip. "As a woman gets older she tends to say what comes to mind 'stead a holdin' back on her tongue. That what you want, James? Me to hold back on you now?"

The last sentence she more spat out than spoke, like a gauntlet thrown to the hard earth.

"No, I guess not," was all Pruett said.

Honey reached across the table and laid her twisted hand atop his. The sweetness of summer nectar returned to her voice. "James. You know how we felt. But we loved you anyway. You're a McIntyre man now. That means somethin' to me. Let it alone. Let this thing go to rest, with our beloved Bethy."

"What about Dirk?"

"Dirk walked out on this family when he walked away from the ranch."

"Dirk's grandfather didn't see it that way, did he?"

"The betrayal of family didn't matter as much to him, I guess. Family is *everything* to me, Sheriff. May not look that way from the outside right now, but damn me straight to Hades if it ain't true. Hell,

Will McIntyre didn't own enough sense to buy himself a coffee. Look at the way he ogled over Ty, the fuckin' misfit."

A look of shock flashed in her coal-colored eyes. "Well excuse my French, James."

"I thought family meant everything," Pruett said.

"Ty'd sell out his family for a bottle of rot gut," she said. "Though I think I still always connected better with his scurrilous kind than any of the others."

"I think you're wrong, ma'am. I think you'd be surprised how much Ty thinks of family. He sure don't take to them murdering each other."

"You was talkin' about a document, I believe: the final Will and whatnot of Rory's pappy," Honey said, lighting a cigarette and drawing until the butt end was red as hellfire. "And the distorted views that man had on who gets what."

"Doesn't matter what his opinions were, Honey," Pruett said. "The law says you divide his assets how he declared they be divided."

"You're talking like I have knowledge of anything being done to the contrary. Illegal things. Things that git people *killed*."

"Bethy's *dead*, Honey."

"And you're her avenger?"

"Goddamn it, Honey, you know too much has happened for me to turn my back on it now."

"Go and grieve, James. Climb back into that bottle you rose out of and just grieve like the rest of us."

"Like you?"

"I don't grieve," Honey said flatly. "The world don't suffer a fool. Grievin' what happened 'cause it needed to happen doesn't change a thing. Waste of time."

"You saying you think Bethy *had* to die?"

"I'm saying the web that gets woven takes on a life of its own. And further ruining the futures of those who are Bethy's flesh and blood won't bring her back."

"Justice will be done," Pruett said. "Whether you help it, ma'am, or hinder it—justice is going to get done."

"More coffee?" Honey said, staring him down with unrepentant eyes.

"Thanks for your hospitality," the sheriff said, taking only his hat with him.

The BLM was one of the most powerful government organizations involved in the affairs of Wyoming and much of the valuable land in the western United States. With an annual budget of almost a billion dollars and producing revenues of six times that number, the BLM was one of the most profitable appendages of a national government that was, in most other agencies, hemorrhaging money.

The bulk of income to the BLM came from the administration of subsurface mineral rights on over seven hundred million acres of land in the United States. These rights were owned on federal, state, and even private lands, depending on historical deeds.

Ty's section of property was one example where land ownership was divided between the person living on the land and the United States government in the form of the BLM.

Sheriff Pruett decided he'd take a drive to Jackson Hole, about seventy miles north and west of Wind River. He drove his personal vehicle—an eighty-nine black Jeep Wrangler—and he wore plain clothing. He didn't intend the trip as official business, at least not outwardly. He wanted to survey the office, see who worked there, and hang around a little just to see why Ty would have left the BLM's phone number carved in his jail cell wall.

Pruett needed to complete some paperwork for the BLM that had to do with the drainage of his property anyway—boilerplate information he could have easily handled at the tiny BLM outpost in Wind River, manned only three days a week, but he was pretty sure none of the answers he was looking for were anyplace but up north in Jackson.

Pruett *did* know that the office in Jackson Hole was bigger and, more importantly, had three or four armed Special Agents working out of that particular location. So if nothing else, it made an obligatory trip to the BLM more interesting.

Pruett figured it meant a hell of a lot more than that, though, and he intended to sniff around as long as he was able.

"May I help you, sir?" the cherubic blonde in standard-issue pea-green BLM button-down asked Pruett as he stepped out of the sunlight and into the coolness of the Jackson Land Management office.

"You surely can," Pruett said. "I have a few acres down south in Sublette County. Filled out this annual drainage report and since I was in Jackson for the day I figured I'd drop it off."

"No problem," the woman said as Pruett handed her the forms.

The Jackson office anteroom was not large but there was one hallway that went back forty or fifty feet with doors on either side.

"Pruett is the surname?" the receptionist said.

"Yes, Ma'am."

A tall man with broad shoulders and tailored suit stepped out of an office behind the receptionist and handed her a folder. He looked up and smiled coolly at Pruett, a flash of recognition in his eyes. Pruett smiled back. He did not recognize the man but from the office layout assumed him to be the Agent in Charge.

"Give these numbers to Mr. Robicheaux from the County Assessor's office when he drops by after lunch. Thanks, Julie."

"Of course, Agent Warren."

Agent Warren spun on a dime and returned to the solitaire of his office while Julie examined the drainage paperwork to ensure everything was in order.

"Do you have a restroom I might use," Pruett asked.

"Certainly. Back down the hallway, last door on the right," said Julie.

Pruett walked back slowly. All the doors were open and the sheriff nodded at a single agent in each of the two offices, both in their twenties, one with bright red hair.

After a cursory visit to the lavatory Pruett returned to the front desk where Julie was smiling and handing him copies of his papers.

"Everything looks just fine, Mr. Pruett. I made copies for your files. Just an FYI, our office in Wind River is open Mondays, Wednesdays, and Fridays for your convenience."

"Mr. Pruett knows that, Julie," Agent Warren said, stepping out of his office, hair parted neatly, teeth chiseled in a federal smile. "He's the sheriff of Wind River if I'm not mistaken."

"Guilty," Pruett said, but did not extend a hand.

"Off-duty it seems today," Warren said curtly.

It was clear the agent wasn't coming any further out into the room nor would he be extending any common courtesy from one law enforcement officer to another.

"Up in Jackson on personal business," Pruett said. "But duty comes in the strangest forms at the most inopportune times, I find."

"You may have heard of James Pruett, Julie. Raised a stir becoming the first black sheriff elected to any township in the great state of Wyoming."

"Just an election," Pruett said. "Though they did charge extra for a viewing in the sideshow tent."

Warren's smile never ceased, nor did it change, as if it really were carved into his jaw. His eyes, however, darkened at the sarcasm. "Funny we've not crossed paths before," he said. "In the line of duty or otherwise, I mean."

"I don't imagine we work the same cases," Pruett said.

"I hope you believe me when I say I feel that's a shame."

"Just when you think they don't, things change," Pruett said. "I thank you, ma'am, for your assistance with these pesky forms. Agent Warren, pleasure to meet you, sir." Pruett tipped his hat.

Neither of them said a word as the sheriff opened the door and squinted at the plume of sunlight.

Hanson was waiting for him in the station when he got back to Wind River. "Don't you answer that cell phone?" Hanson said.

Pruett pulled the phone from his pocket. "Dead."

"Beulah Jorgensen didn't show up for the proceedings this morning," Hanson told him.

"Shit."

"Your deputies already checked her house and of course the Town Attorney's office."

"No luck," Pruett said.

"None. Where've you been?"

"I had business in Jackson Hole. When's the last time you saw Beulah?" Pruett said.

"In court yesterday afternoon."

"What happens now with the trial?"

"The judge ordered Miles Stanton to take over the prosecution until Beulah can be located. Gave him a continuance until Monday morning.

"That gives us a couple days and the weekend to turn up your prosecutor."

"I won't be holding my breath," said Hanson.

"You ever hear of cops having 'gut reactions'?"

"Yep."

"We need to make a visit to an old friend of mine."

Pruett took Hanson to Jesse Claremont's house. He knocked on the door but no one was home. Jesse had gotten her teaching job back at the middle school a few years ago. He realized it was just after four—yes, the kids were out for the day, but Jesse was likely still at the school working on papers or on Friday's lesson plan.

They found her sitting behind the large desk at the front of her classroom, reading glasses perched atop her slightly upturned nose— the one the sheriff had kissed lightly before saying goodbye just two mornings prior. She looked over the top of those glasses, azure eyes lighting up almost imperceptibly upon recognizing him.

"Sheriff Pruett," she said.

"Jesse. Meet Jay Hanson. He's Ty's attorney."

Hanson stepped forward and Jesse rose to shake his hand. "I know who he is," she said warmly. "I think it's a good thing, what you're doing here, sir."

"Jay, please."

"Okay, Jay."

"I want you to tell Jay what you told me the other night," Pruett said.

"Sorry?"

"It's okay, Jess. Hanson and me, we've talked a bit. About the booze; about a lot of things."

"Oh."

"Beulah Jorgensen has gone missing," he told her.

"When?"

"She didn't show up for court today," Hanson said. "She was there yesterday afternoon."

"You thinking she's with Rory?" Jesse said to Pruett.

Hanson looked from one to the other.

"Tell him," Pruett said.

"Beulah and Rory McIntyre have been carrying on an affair for the better part of a year," she said. "There's a cabin up at Timber Lake. It's where they meet."

"How do you know all this," Hanson said, dumbfounded.

"Beulah and I used to drink together," she said. "I've been dry a year and a half longer than her."

"You're her sponsor," Hanson said.

"She tells me everything, especially about her love life."

"You'd have made a terrible lawyer," Hanson said.

"I take my sponsor relationship seriously, Mr. Hanson. But murder trumps that in my book."

"I actually meant it as a compliment," Hanson said, smiling.

"The McIntyres have no cabin I know of," said Pruett. "Can you tell us where this one is?"

Jesse shook her head. "Not where, but who. It's owned by some people from Rock Springs. Name is Townsley."

"I know that cabin," Pruett said to Hanson. "It's a bit further up on the lake, near a place called Gentry Bay."

"You think that's where she is?" Hanson said.

"Didn't see Rory when I was out at the ranch."

"You said it yourself, they're always out on the land working."

"What I didn't remember until a little while ago is that I saw his truck at the hardware store on my way back into town."

Pruett pointed to Jesse's cell phone. "Mine's dead, may I?"

He called the station and told Baptiste and Munney to meet him at the turnout above the lake.

Rory's truck was at the cabin as was Beulah Jorgensen's small Toyota Prius. But there was no activity at all. The driveway wound inward through a series of switchbacks that came into view several times; a clandestine approach wasn't possible unless you planned on walking the mile in from the main road, using the thick lodgepole pine as cover. Pruett didn't. Rory and Beulah weren't dangerous suspects in his book. Assholes, yes, but not all that threatening.

Baptiste and Munney stood on either side of the sheriff at the bottom of the porch steps. Pruett climbed stiffly to the front door and rapped on it loudly.

"Rory. Beulah. Give us a moment of your time," he called out.

Nothing.

He rapped a little harder this time.

Still nothing.

Pruett tried the knob and found it unlocked.

"You hear that cry for help?" he said and un-holstered his gun.

"I did," said Munney. She was already armed.

Red Horse Baptiste nodded and pulled his weapon, too.

They both climbed the stairs and entered with their sheriff.

The house was still, not well lit. They allowed their eyes to adjust before moving further into the residence. The three split in different directions and began clearing the structure room by room.

Pruett found the victims tied together in the bedroom. They'd each been shot, Beulah Jorgensen multiple times. Rory was clothed, but his shirt and jeans were tattered and ripped to pieces—barely hanging about his bruised, scarred, and bloodied body. There was one large caliber hole in the back of his head but it would take the coroner to determine whether it was the bullet or being dragged behind some kind of vehicle that caused the death.

Pruett knew the McIntyre's too well; mercy wasn't likely in the cards. Still he wished silently that the bullet killed the elder McIntyre before they dragged him all over sagebrush country because to imagine the suffering inflicted on Rory before he died was otherwise too awful.

Beulah was stripped naked, and though she'd not been dragged as had her lover, her pale, mottled body was anything but pristine— she'd clearly been beaten around the chest, shoulders, and face, and there were multiple gunshot wounds in her center mass. Looked like a different caliber than the weapon used on Rory; the entry wounds were significantly smaller. A .22, perhaps.

A woman's gun.

However the scenarios played out, and by whom, both of them died hard and whoever killed each of them did so with malice, purpose, succumbing to the hunger of vengeance.

When they'd cleared the rest of the house, Pruett's deputies joined him.

"Call it in," Pruett said. "And get the others up here."

"Yessir," Munney said and went outside to the Suburban.

"Looks like our killers made this personal," Baptiste said.

"A lot of people took exception to the both of 'em," Pruett said. "But this went beyond 'personal'. This was *family*."

The sheriff went outside to talk with Hanson.

"I can't let you in there," he told the lawyer.

"Understood."

"Never much cared for either of 'em, but no one deserves *that*."

"You've not seen worse?"

"Not outside the borders of war, I haven't."

"You seem troubled. Beyond the obvious, I mean."

"Well I gotta tell my little girl her grandfather's been murdered."

"Were they close?" Hanson said.

"Not particularly. But you know Wendy. She loves people unconditionally."

"She loves you like that, too."

"So it seems," Pruett said. "I'm going to drop you off in town. Then I'm gonna pick up Honey McIntyre for questioning."

On the way back into Wind River a thought suddenly occurred to the sheriff. "What're they going to do about the trial?"

Hanson shook his head. "This is a strange one," he said. "I already started writing a motion asking for a new prosecuting attorney. Miles Stanton is the only lawyer in that office left standing. We can inform the judge together in chambers and request a continuance. Under these circumstances I think Butler would consider a mistrial."

"Let me think about it," Pruett said. "I don't want this getting talked about all over the streets of town. Not yet."

"I can call a meeting in Judge's chambers. We can request the facts be contained for a few days. Enough time for you to put some of these pieces together."

"Good. You familiar with the BLM?"

"Only from half of my Wyoming History class."

"Things are bigger here than I feared. The reach of this thing goes outside this county."

"I'll ask Butler for more time," Hanson said. "I want you there in chambers if he has any questions I can't answer," Hanson said. He pulled his cell from his pocket and called Miles Stanton. He then called Judge Butler. Pruett listened to him set up the meeting and thought about how he was going to tell Wendy she'd lost a third relative and then how a drink sounded better than any other thing at that moment.

"Sitting by a foggy window
Staring at the pouring rain
Falling down like lonely teardrops
Memories of love in vain
These cloudy days,
make you wanna cry
It breaks your heart
when someone leaves
and you don't know why."

The Eagles,
No More Cloudy Days

Chapter 16

WENDY DIDN'T say anything for a long while. Pruett respected her silence, waiting patiently for whatever her reaction might be. Hanson had waited outside at the sheriff's request. When his daughter finally spoke, Pruett then found *he* didn't know how to answer after all.

"Why does it have to come down so hard, all at once?" she said.

"The rain?"

"Yes."

"I don't know, girl. I really don't. Sometimes our number gets called and the heavens just open up."

"This seems a lot more like Hell," Wendy said.

"That it does."

"I always liked Uncle Ty," she said. "Never was close to granddad."

"No."

"But I still don't understand. I thought he was your suspect."

"Things get murkier the further down we've gone," the sheriff said. "I don't like what we're turning up. Some ways I'm glad your mother isn't here to witness it."

"Are the McIntyres really this bad?" Wendy said.

"Not all the way," he said. "Mainly 'cause your mother was one of 'em. And for all his ranting and surliness, Ty is a rough package but I'd say he's not too far past half bad."

"How many others are involved?" Wendy said.

"That's what I aim to find out next. Bringing Honey and the other two boys in for questioning. After the meeting with the judge."

"I'm sorry," she said.

"Sorry for what?"

"That you have to deal with your town coming apart when you need to be concentrating on yourself. Your own grieving."

"I'll be okay. Makes me want to take a sip something fierce but I also like the challenge of it. Keepin' it from beating me, you know?"

"I do know."

"I just wish I'd realized all this sooner, maybe if I had…"

"You couldn't have," she said and put her hand on his. "No one could."

"It's gonna get dark, girl. A lot more before it gets light again."

Judge Butler didn't like the new turn of events. He was even more inclined to call a mistrial than Hanson had predicted. He looked to the sheriff for answers. "What the hell is going on here, James?"

"Bridger, you know as well as I do that we're just starting to piece this shit together."

"It would be helpful deciding how to proceed if the puzzle were finished."

"Yessir, I understand that."

Butler looked at Miles Stanton, who gave the appearance of a schoolchild waiting to give his first recital. The weight of the Universe had just dropped on the shoulders of a twenty-seven year-old kid a year and a half out of law school. "I'm about to ask you if after a reasonable continuance you'll be prepared to take the reins on this case and drive 'er home. Don't tell me no, son. Don't you even think about doing that."

"Nossir," Stanton said.

"You'll be ready?"

"Nossir—I mean, Yessir. Yes, sir. I'll be ready to proceed, Judge."

"Good," Butler said. He turned to Hanson. "Two weeks. It's all I can manage without shutting this whole thing down."

"It'll have to do then," Hanson said.

"We'll convene in the morning to make this a matter of the official record," Butler said.

"Can we keep the specifics off the record for now?" Pruett said.

"For *now*," the judge replied. "Reconvene at nine A.M. for issuance on the record."

Pruett left the chambers and said goodbye to Hanson. His intent was to drive out to the McIntyre ranch and haul Honey and whoever else was there in for questioning. He felt it was time to let her know he wasn't backing down.

He didn't make it.

For some reason he'd been thinking about Jesse all morning. Since seeing all that death again. In addition to making him long for a drink, he also craved some human contact. Not the kind he was in store for with the McIntyres—he needed something that made him feel *alive*.

The booze promised that but never really delivered. He'd feel alive for a short while—as if he were firing on all cylinders—but that was vaporous at best. He needed something that would fuel him for the long run. Or at least more than a few hours.

Jesse could do that for him. And she was sober. Maybe *she* could be his sponsor. He knew that was a horrible idea (and not entirely appropriate), but she was someone he trusted and, yes, probably even loved a little.

He ached then, as if a small pebble of guilt had just caught in the side of his heart. He thought of Bethy again. What he'd done to her trust all those years back. Thoughts of his own failure and betrayal were never more than a few feet from center stage, just waiting in the wings for their chance to jump into the spotlight.

No one blamed him more or was less forgiving than he was to himself. No one. But even back then he knew he loved Jesse. Not in the same way he loved his wife—his love for Bethy was rock solid; it was the kind of love that was a foundation for greater things. The cornerstone of an entire life spent together, being there for each other, helping one another. Until death do us part.

Death.

It took the death of his beloved to wrench her away from his life. The love he felt for Jesse was different. More raw and exposed—less healthy for him, like the booze.

No. That wasn't fair. Jesse was not bad for him. She was not an addiction either. But still the love was different. That didn't make him need it any less. At that moment Pruett felt like he needed the warmth of human contact more than ever before in his life. He wanted to curl into a tiny ball and cry like a baby.

Pruett didn't cry. Or at least he rarely did. Not since he came back from the war. He saw far too many tears there to ever want to cry any himself again.

But now he wanted to. Needed to.

And in Jesse's arms he could do that.

He could cry.

Judge Butler convened trial Monday morning in order to grant the motion for continuance. It had been agreed in chambers the prosecution would first put the change of counsel into the record and after it being so ordered would then submit the motion for a two-week continuance.

"Mr. Stanton, I understand you are proposing to take over the case from Ms. Jorgensen, is this correct?" Judge Butler said to the prosecutor.

"Yes, Your Honor," Stanton said. "I filed the official paperwork this morning before court."

"So ordered."

"Thank you, Judge."

"You also have a motion for continuance before the court."

"Yes. Due to exigent circumstances the State feels it needs some extra time to, uh, familiarize with the case." Stanton looked nervous, even though he knew he'd get his continuance.

"Two weeks should suffice, I would think," Butler said.

"Yes, sir. Two weeks is good."

"Any objections from the defense table, Mr. Hanson?"

"None, Your Honor."

"Court will then reconvene…"

The two main doors to the courtroom exploded open at the same time, both doors behind the bench opened quickly and two armed men with jean jackets and black ski masks slipped in behind Judge Butler. One put the muzzle of a side-by-side shotgun against the judge's throat while the other disarmed the bailiff and tied his wrists behind him with zip-tie cuffs.

Two other men, one armed with two 9mm pistols and the other with a pump action shotgun and a silver .38 caliber stuffed in his belt, stormed down the aisle, controlling the crowd. Both had similar ski masks. The one with the two pistols came straight for Pruett, one barrel pointed between the sheriff's eyes.

"Off with that gun belt, Sheriff," the man said, trying to keep his voice gruff and unrecognizable.

"Fuck you, Rance," Pruett said and spat on the floor. "Yeah, I know it's you. You going to shoot me here in front of all these witnesses, are ya?"

"I said the gun belt or I put a hole in ya the size a Kansas, old man."

"My hands will stay where you see them, but I won't disarm myself. Not here. Not ever."

"Drop one a them hands a fox hair, Sheriff and you'll be sorry."

Pruett kept his eyes locked on Rance McIntyre's. The cowpoke looked scared. Like he'd already failed part of the plan and was now busy calculating what would go wrong next.

What went wrong next didn't take all that long.

LaRue Hilton was an old rancher whose family had lived in the Green River valley since long before Wyoming was anything but Indian territory. One of the true pioneers of the land. He was eighty-nine years young and as ornery as any man in Wind River. He was also a friend of Judge Butler. Their families had been intertwined since LaRue could remember and he wasn't going to miss his friend presiding over the trial of the century.

Like many other residents of Wind River (and of Wyoming in general), LaRue was armed. He was armed when he picked up his groceries, armed at the Post Office mailing letters to his granddaughters in Spokane and Hurt, Texas, and he was damn sure armed that day in court.

And he didn't care for seeing his friend sweating bullets because of a side-by-side Winchester pressed up into the folds of his neck. LaRue eased the Colt Navy .38 out of the holster slung over his frail shoulder and strapped to his chest. He was a crack shot with that pistol and had a clear line on the back of the masked man behind the bench. He looked over at the two men to his rear and they were busy controlling the crowd, not paying attention to some old geezer down at the end of the front gallery. LaRue decided God wasn't going to give him another opportunity to do the right thing

The old man stood and pointed the Colt at the back of the masked man's head and he pulled back the hammer. "Don't move, you fucking *shit*," LaRue said.

For Pruett the whole room slowed down at that moment. He'd caught the movement in his peripheral when old Long Pole LaRue came to his feet, gun drawn, and he knew there wasn't going to be any time to undo the ugliness that was about to unfold. He'd seen it too many times—it was one thing when you had a standoff with a bunch of well-trained participants. But this small handful of

McIntyres and God knew who else were about as nervous as you ever wanted to see armed men with guns be.

The man with the shotgun pressed into Judge Butler would later be identified as Carter Lee Holcomb through examining the remaining third of his face. In the movies when a suspect hears something like "freeze" or "don't move, you *shit*" they don't make a move, unless it's to put their weapon down or raise their hands dutifully in the air. In the real world a gunman like Carter Lee Holcomb isn't considered "dangerous" because he's armed—it's mostly because he's cagey and stupid and probably more than a little bit tuned up on whatever poison he thinks puts courage in his veins.

Carter Lee heard LaRue's command all right but he damn sure didn't comply. Holcomb spun (in slow motion, or at least that's how Sheriff Pruett saw it all go down) and just got the loaded barrels halfway to LaRue when the first .38 slug tore off all of his cheek and the top half of his skull.

The concussion was so profound it spun Carter Lee back around, like a lifeless side of beef doing an awkward pirouette. Judge Butler just missed being the second gruesome casualty of the morning when he dropped to his knees and the blast of Holcomb's shotgun shaved the top of his thinning hair—the gun having gone off by the death spasm that contracted Carter Lee's finger on the hair trigger.

Rance McIntyre had let himself get caught up in the action at the front of the courtroom—like a man drawn into a television program, where everything else around him goes dim. And it was only for a second or two. But when he turned back toward the sheriff, his eyes had a fear in them that meant he'd just realized even a second or two was too much, and that he'd lost the upper hand.

Pruett already had his revolver leveled on McIntyre and before Rance could get even one of his barrels turned on the sheriff, the lawman put three slugs into the man's heart.

Pruett looked up front in time to see the remaining two gunmen running with a handcuffed Ty McIntyre between them, exiting out the judge's private hallway, where there was a rarely used exit to the rear of the courthouse.

"Need an ambulance and all officers to respond at the County Courthouse," the sheriff said into his shoulder mic. "Shots fired, two perps down. Maybe more civilians. Two suspects have Ty McIntyre and are leaving out the back of the courthouse."

Pruett put up his free hand and tried to calm the crowd. "Everyone, please, quiet down. Stay where you are. If you can sit, SIT. Do not try to leave."

The sheriff walked slowly over to the body of Rance McIntyre and felt for a pulse. He then walked down the aisle to the front of the courtroom. Carter Lee Holcomb was clearly dead. He was missing more than half his head. Pruett looked around, scanning for other injuries. He couldn't be sure how many shots he'd heard.

Several townsfolk tended to LaRue Hilton, who had taken a slug in the shoulder from the assailant closest to the deputy—one of the two who had escaped.

Having determined there were no other injuries, Pruett ran for the back hallway where the men who abducted his prisoner had escaped.

Pruett called in the Wyoming Highway Patrol to assist in roadblocks going south to Rock Springs and northwest toward Jackson Hole, Yellowstone, Idaho, and Star Valley. The problem wasn't the highways. There had to be eight or nine different county roads that headed to the mesa or to half a dozen lakes and mountainous areas surrounding Wind River. And from most of those locations fugitives from the law could get just about anywhere else in the county they needed to, as long as they had a decent knowledge of the area.

They canvassed the town but no one saw the kidnappers leave the courthouse.

And Pruett *was* calling it a kidnapping. It was no jailbreak. If they didn't find Ty soon, he'd be as dead as the rest of the bodies that were piling up. If he wasn't dead already.

Back at the station Pruett found himself alone. He walked back to Ty's cell. He saw Ty's face as the masked gunmen were hauling him from the courtroom. He hadn't looked surprised at all. Was it possible; could it really have been a jailbreak? Pruett still didn't think so. But there was something else. Something in the prisoner's demeanor. As if he'd known it was just a matter of time.

Pruett stared into Ty McIntyre's empty cell. A pile of Zane Grey novels the sheriff had borrowed from the library after Ty declared his hatred of Louis L'Amour. He walked into the cell and dropped down on the cot, nearly busting the legs out from under.

"DAMN it," Pruett breathed. Killing in war was inevitable. That didn't make it much better, but at least there was a plausible answer for it. But all this death here, in his own town—his quiet, peaceful, decent town? Pruett hadn't seen but one murder in his tenure as a law officer in Wind River. One murder in thirty-five years. Now he had four bodies down at the morgue. Five if he counted Bethy.

Six if he didn't get to them before they executed his prisoner.

Pruett knew Ty was telling him something. How exactly the BLM played into the mess that had unfolded and was threatening the sheriff's own town was unclear but Pruett decided he should pay another visit to Ty's ranch house and attempt to locate that damn lockbox.

The sheriff went alone. Most folks didn't realize the power of the Bureau. To most the BLM was a kind of lame duck organization that monitored the parks, open prairies, fed the feral horses and wintering elk, and most importantly funded the brave firefighters who battled the wildfires each summer.

But the Bureau did more than manage; they *enforced*. Special Agents for the BLM were armed, plain-clothed law enforcement personnel that conducted criminal investigations, served warrants, made arrests, and policed the internal regulatory concerns of the organization itself, presenting cases to the U.S. Attorney directly.

Sheriff Pruett knew one such agent, based in the Kemmerer office—and old friend named Barry Fielding—and he figured he might just have to make a call to his compadre once he figured out how the BLM figured into the killings in Wind River.

Ty's house had been ransacked. Pruett's deputies hadn't much reason to search Ty's home after Bethy's death. The crime occurred twenty miles away and the murder weapon had been on his person when arrested. The only other visit law enforcement personnel had made to Ty's residence was the night the sheriff and Deputy Baptiste recovered the slug meant for the cowpoke's skull, and the house had looked fine then.

It was clear someone else was interested in finding something there, too. Pruett couldn't explain it by anything more than gut instinct, but he felt Ty's message to him was meant to cause more than an errant call to the BLM office in Jackson Hole. Ty was mean as a cornered badger but he wasn't stupid. Pruett had known from the start that his prisoner was withholding information and he'd also known Ty would divulge it when he was damn good and ready—or better, when it benefitted his own self.

And if Ty had gotten wind of what was going down in the courtroom that morning, this might have been his last chance to get the clue to the only man in Wind River still willing to help him.

Now the sheriff had to wonder what good he could do and what he had any chance of finding. Whoever had searched the house before him had turned it upside down and inside out. Every drawer was opened and dumped on the floor; cushions were cut wide and the stuffing pulled; loose floorboards had been pried up and the cavities beneath them searched.

The scene looked professionally executed. Not the ragtag search of a few half-drunk ranch hands. Whoever had been looking through Ty's house knew what the hell they were doing. They'd been *trained* to conduct such searches.

Pruett thought about his next move. Such an exhaustive search meant they likely didn't find what they were looking for. It wasn't guaranteed by any means, but if they found what they wanted it had to have been in one of the last places they looked. Again, unlikely.

So what did Pruett know about his brother-in-law that a gaggle of flunky federal agents didn't know?

The Willow Saloon was nearly empty; just a few broken-down regulars drinking away their government disability checks and mortgage payments. Roland Pape sat behind the bar, reading a newspaper, and gnawing on a toothpick that looked like it'd been mashed with a pair of flat-nosed pliers.

"Sheriff," Pape said.

"Roland."

"What can I do you for?"

"Fill me up a glass of soda water," Pruett said. "Put a little cherry juice in it for me and keep the smart ass comments to yourself."

"How's Ty holdin' up?" Pape said as he made the sheriff's drink.

"You heard about what happened?"

"I heard. Just makin' conversation."

"I need to ask you a question," Pruett said. "And you need to know Ty's life probably depends heavily on the answer."

Pape handed the sheriff the glass and nodded. "Sounds serious."

"Ty ever ask you to keep anything for him?"

"Like what?"

"See, Roland, that's exactly the kind of cat and mouse shit Ty ain't got time for. Me and you, sure, we've got all the time in the world. But Ty, his clock's ticking, old man. Answer the fucking question."

"No. Ty never gave me nothin'."

"Thank you for your time, then," Pruett said. He left the cherry fizz untouched.

As he walked to the door he put his hat on and then stopped. "It won't take long for the men who tore his house apart to figure out what I figured out. When they do, they'll come callin'. My advice is to get in some target practice. You never were any good with that scatter gun behind the bar."

Pruett left the bar and walked down the steps to the Suburban. Roland Pape flagged him down as he was starting to pull out of the parking lot. The sheriff rolled down the window.

"This lockbox," Pape said, sweating and out of breath. "He gave me this the night before he shot, well, the night before he got locked up. Said no one would be the wiser and he'd get it back when he was sprung."

He handed the shoebox-sized lockbox to Pruett.

"Washin' my hands of it now," Pape said. "You make sure you tell whoever's lookin' for it that I ain't got it no more. You do that, Sheriff?"

Pruett rolled up the window and sped away, leaving Roland Pape in a cloud of dirt, gravel, and bewildered silence.

He called J.W. Hanson on his way back to town.

"I have something you need to see," Pruett told him.

"What kind of something?"

"The kind hidden in a fireproof lockbox your client saw fit to hide with a third party before his incarceration."

"That sounds like an important something."

"You'd find me in agreement," Pruett said. "Also the kind of something that's been getting people murdered, I'd say."

"I hate to sound disingenuous, but is there a reason you called me?"

"Deciding who to trust has recently become a tough proposition."

"I'll take that as a compliment."

"Meet me at my house?" Pruett said.

"And Wendy?"

"I'd prefer she know as little as possible about this business. Might keep her safe."

"Agreed. See you in a half hour," Hanson said.

"Make it two hours," Pruett said. "I have one stop to make."

The sheriff drove down to the south end of town and turned into the driveway of one Malcolm Whitefeather. In addition to being one of James Pruett's oldest friends—one of the lucky soldiers who returned with Jimmy Pruett from the jungles of Asia—Whitefeather worked twenty-two years in the Colorado Bureau of Investigations special bomb unit.

As a child Whitefeather had been misdiagnosed as a pyromaniac. It turns out the boy just liked to blow shit up. The incident in question was a house fire on the Wind River Indian Reservation that resulted in a complete loss of structure (and luckily, no lives). The investigators determined the fire had been set at the rear external of the house—a common location for arsonists to set their fire without having to risk entry into the property.

Malcolm Whitefeather, nine at the time, was charged as a minor—several witnesses had seen the young Indian boy running from the scene. The accelerant used was ruled as gasoline. Just before trial Whitefeather's mother had convinced him to tell the truth about the incident:

Little Malcolm and a friend (who happened to live at the torched home) had forged several sticks of what they thought would be homemade dynamite but were really only plastic plumbing pipes filled with a mixture of gasoline, lard, frozen orange juice, and Epsom salt.

After accidently lighting one makeshift stick, the boys panicked and ran. The fumes in the nearby gas tank exploded, not the useless sticks of dynamite—however, the gasoline mixture showered the side of the house and acted like napalm, setting the entire house ablaze in moments.

Whitefeather didn't need to be drafted; he *joined* the Army, where testing showed his aptitude for (and interest in) explosives. He was assigned to Jimmy Pruett's platoon as one of three demolition experts. After the war, PFC Whitefeather finished his Criminal Justice degree on the GI Bill and joined the CBI.

"What do you have there, Jimmy?" Whitefeather said, sitting on the wood deck sipping his own private concoction of herbal tea.

"Morning to you, too, Mal," Pruett said, carrying the box in front of him, as he had since retrieving it from Roland Pape. "Somethin' I need you to look over for me."

Whitefeather set down his tea and rose stiffly from the chair. "Arthritis," he said. "It's a fucking bear. Scratch that. I'd *rather* take on a bear. These days don't feel like I could take on a blind alley cat. Declawed."

Pruett set the lockbox on the small round deck table.

"Ain't been opened, I take it," Whitefeather said, his eyes already alive with the dance. He looked like a kid who just got his birthday present a day early.

"Not by me," Pruett said. "My feeling is there's some important evidence in there."

"Important enough to incinerate whatever's inside?"

"Important enough to incinerate whoever's *outside*," Pruett said.

Whitefeather turned the box carefully, examining the external—feeling the weight of it as it lay on the palms of his opened hands.

He set it back down on the table.

"It's probably good you stuck to paved roads in coming out here," Whitefeather said.

"How do you know what roads I took in getting here?"

"'Cause had ya driven too far down any of the shitty county roads, that lid coulda busted real good and you'd be nothin' but chunks of bone, guts, blood, and dust."

"Jesus Christ."

"Whosever box you've got here wasn't fuckin' around, Jimmy. You want my best guess, based on weight, and what I know about fits in a box this size? If there's something in there, it's an S-mine."

"S-mine?"

"Sorry. Bouncing Betty. Well, a knockoff, likely. The Finns and French both attempted to copy the German mine, but failed. The Ruskies, however, made a much simpler, smaller version that would fit nicely into a box about this size. German model was too bulky."

"Goddamn. How the hell do we get it open?" Pruett said.

Whitefeather slowly turned the box around and pointed to a heavy patch of rust. Pruett squinted but had to pull out his reading glasses. It was then he saw it.

A small drilled hole hidden in the orange rust.

Just big enough for a trigger pin.

"You open this up without the pin…" Whitefeather said.

"I get it."

Pruett had seen enough men blown to bits by Bettys during his tours. The lucky ones anyway. The unlucky ones only got themselves half blown up—maybe both arms, or their entire lower half. Those men earned themselves a few minutes of confused agony, wondering how the hell parts of them ended up over there on that rock or up those branches in that tree.

"Come out to the workshop," Whitefeather said.

The old bomb man had several boxes of disarmed explosive devices in various states of deconstruction. In a junk drawer that looked like it belonged to the Unabomber, Whitefeather scrounged a handful of different sized trigger pins. "I have no idea what the Russian pin looks like," he said. "If we're lucky, there's a match here."

"And if not?"

"You know where the owner of this box is?"

"We're workin' on that," Pruett said.

Out on the porch the old Indian laid the half-dozen pins in one organized pile on the table. One by one he slowly inserted them into the hole. "What I'm looking for," he said quietly, his face brown and crinkled in concentration, "is a firm match. The correct pin should slide in nice and snug and snap into place. Problem is, I can't see the hole."

"So it either works or it doesn't, right?"

"One of these pins gets jammed in there just right, it'd be like breaking a key off in a deadlock. And there'd be no guarantee at all that the trigger had gotten blocked."

"Shit."

Whitefeather kept working and Pruett kept sweating. More than once the old sheriff glanced sideways for his unopened bottle of Heaven.

Five and a half days. Not six.

Five and a half.

And as God would have it, the sixth pin slid snugly and clicked perfectly into place.

"That's as disarmed as it's going to get, Jimmy."

"Are we safe?"

"We had a saying we'd give to the newbies in the unit: if you're looking for safety, go climb Mount Everest. This is here is the *bomb squad*, son."

Pruett looked into his old friend's eyes.

"Get the fuck outta here, Mal. This isn't your scrape."

"You take out my home you might as well take me with it," he said, a pearly white smile stretching wide. "Besides. I put that pin in there. Even amongst friends, trust should only be expected to run so deep."

Pruett took a calming breath. Rivulets of sweat were raining down his face.

"You have the combination?" Whitefeather said.

"Pretty sure."

"Do it, then."

Pruett thumbed the wheels until they read 7002499, left to right. He looked at Whitefeather, who was staring at the soaked brim of the sheriff's hatband.

"The secrets of my wife's murder are likely inside this box."

"You familiar with the story of Pandora?" Whitefeather said.

"Why do you think I'm sweating so hard?" said Pruett.

"'Cause you're either gonna find them secrets or you're goin' to find *her*."

"Amen," said Pruett.

He pressed the rust-spattered lever down and the small deadbolt clicked audibly. He never doubted it would.

Pruett steadied himself and looked at Whitefeather for the go-ahead.

Whitefeather smiled and nodded; he looked like he was waiting for the songbird on the end of the porch to pick her next tune. The old Indian picked up his herbal tea and took a sip. The cup wasn't shaking at all.

Pruett slowly lifted the lid. The hinges creaked loudly and scared away the bird. The sheriff almost pissed himself. Whitefeather took another sip.

As the lid opened fully, the two men saw exactly what they expected to see: a fairly new Russian OMZ-72, snugged against the side of the lockbox with two heavy Velcro straps.

Alongside the mine were a pile of folded papers, envelopes, and what looked like a padlock key. There was nothing beneath the mine; it rested snugly on the bottom of the box.

"I want this thing disposed of," Pruett said. "And that's all I can tell you about the situation."

"I'd take those papers and things out of there, then, and we'll take 'er out back in the trees and make sure this bitch never hurts anyone ever again," said Whitefeather.

Pruett gathered all the contents and they closed the lockbox tightly again. Whitefeather led the sheriff around back where they walked a hundred yards into the dense pine forest.

The Indian knelt and with his hands clawed out a small hole up against a giant rock that was three-quarters underground.

"Place it in there; make sure I can still reach the pin. That boulder'll help contain the blast and the trees will absorb the bulk of the shrapnel."

Pruett placed the box backwards in the hole. Whitefeather waved him back and then slowly removed the safety trigger.

The two men double-timed it back to the house and Whitefeather brought out his .280 Remington.

"It don't look like much," Whitefeather said. "But it's a sweet little game rifle. Bagged me a deer and a cow elk last year, one clean shot each."

As he spoke he removed the standard cartridges he kept loaded in it and placed them gently, methodically into a box of similar shells. When he had completely unloaded the weapon he set aside the ammo carton and reached into his shirt pocket, producing a bullet that looked as if it were made from silver, so smooth, glistening, and perfect it was.

"Hunting werewolves?" Pruett said.

"It ain't silver," Whitefeather told him as he chambered the one round. "Nickel-plated brass. I like stuff that's harder to find and beautiful. Like us Indians."

Pruett smiled. "And that slug," he said, pointing to the bluish tip on the ammunition.

"Incendiary tip," Whitefeather said. "Makes a nice little explosion. Fun for beer cans and such."

"Or Bouncing Bettys."

"Among other things," he said, and handed Pruett a pair of earmuffs. "Even at this distance, your ear drums are gonna thank you."

Pruett put on the headgear, as did Whitefeather. The old Blackfoot rested the barrel of the Remington on a tree branch and looked through the scope. Without taking his eye off the target he said, "You sure about this, Sheriff?"

"Yep," Pruett said, and Whitefeather squeezed off the round.

Both men had seen battle and both of them had witnessed countless explosions, from mortar rounds to hand grenades to every kind of shoebox bomb ever built. But you never got used to the profundity of a detonation. Like a car crash. People saw them all the time on television, and may have even been involved in one when they were younger and forgotten. But that sound of metal on metal, of glass imploding or exploding—there was nothing like it in the world.

And there was nothing like an honest to God Betty when she let loose her fury. No man or woman ever got used to that kind of sheer force, nor the thought that always followed:

What if that'd been ME?

Pruett took the papers, envelopes, maps, and small ledger and drove not toward his own home but toward Timber Lake and the Townsley cabin. He had rethought everything after seeing the complexity of the weapon in that lock box. The detonation in the forest behind Malcolm Whitefeather's place had awakened the soldier in him. Pruett felt alive again. His senses danced and tingled. He felt as if he could see a thousand miles in all directions.

His own property wasn't safe. He didn't fear for Hanson, not yet, but he needed to get word to him and, more importantly, he needed to bring his daughter to him. The tactician in him said the last place anyone would look, place a wire, or watch would be the Rory McIntyre murder scene.

He avoided town and any of the primary roads. He had the element of surprise and he intended to keep it as long as possible. Clearly whoever opened that lockbox would have died—vaporized along with every shred of evidence that made the truth plausible. Ty would have already been tortured into telling Warren about the explosive trap, his carving of the numbers, and his assumption that Pruett had gotten to the box. Pruett hoped that meant Warren assumed his job had been accomplished for him, as to getting rid of the sheriff.

Pruett had made certain he wasn't followed to the Whitefeather property. He also kept his wits about him and made certain there wasn't anyone surveilling the Townsley property (although that required him hiding the Suburban down a secondary cabin driveway and hiking a mile of stealth approach through the trees and hillsides).

Once inside the cabin, Pruett's cell phone chirped and he froze. He flipped it open and stared at it like he was the first man to discover fire. He silently cursed himself for shunning technology. He brought up the text-messaging screen, where there was an incoming message from J.W. Hanson's cell number. He frowned when he read the message:

Changing meet. Saw two dark vehicles parked on your road, just sitting around. Lookouts. Can we meet at the Townsley cabin?

Pruett had no idea if text messages could be tapped or not

He replied:

Done. Make sure you're not FOLLOWED.

Understood. Wendy's at the hotel, napping. We're good.

Pruett then dialed a different number on his phone. "Are you organized?" he said to the voice on the other end of the line.

After hearing what he needed, Pruett climbed back into the trees. His gut told him things had gone sour and the preferred vantage point was from above. But he checked his cell phone and had lost all but one lousy signal bar. If he had to give the go-ahead…

A black SUV that looked Government-issued eventually came rolling down the drive toward the Townsley cabin. He couldn't see through the opaque windows but he now worried who might be inside. The timing was off. If things were off-schedule that meant anything was possible. It meant his gut was right and things had gone fiercely wrong.

Malcolm Whitefeather had given the sheriff a pair of M33 fragmentation grenades and a Claymore, the combination of which was meant to constitute Plan B. Of course there really was no Plan A. Pruett figured on working one out with Hanson, legal-like.

Plan B was one of the first things he learned in the Army. Their drill sergeant would say "Set up a perimeter of C4 and a couple of claymore tripwires for Plan B."

Some scrotum-head would inevitably ask "what's Plan A, Sarge?"

The DI's answer was always the same: "Don't have one yet, numb nuts. But blowin' shit up is *always* Plan B. You bring Plan B to weddings, bar mitzvahs, and even the fucking ice cream social when we get in the shit. Got it, son?"

Pruett had no desire for the enacting of Plan B, especially if his daughter was amongst the passenger list of the big Expedition coming to a stop sixty yards away from his concealed position.

Pruett took a breath and willed his nervous system to throttle itself down. If Wendy was in that vehicle there could be no Plan B and that's all there was to it. He looked down at his cell phone, moved it around for a better signal. He typed in the message, ready, just waiting for him to press 'send'.

The doors to the vehicle below opened up and two tall, broad-shouldered men who could have been twins except one was dark-haired and the other a redhead stepped out of the driver door and a passenger door, same side. The twins were also clearly Government issue, bulges in their breasts and ankles. No other doors were opened and no one else showed their person.

"Come out, Sheriff," Carrot-top shouted. "Whatever you're thinking, it's not going to happen."

Cocky bastards, Pruett thought. *I'll give 'em that.* The sheriff moved quietly, trying to find a signal. And where was Hanson? In the Expedition? With his daughter?

Wendy was in that truck. Intuition told him it wasn't Hanson who texted him. Hanson was dead. Or worse. Pruett's world was unraveling.

For now he waited. Buying minutes only, he knew, but every minute would count from there on in.

Carrot-top motioned to the SUV. The other man opened a door, pulled down the middle seat, and yanked Wendy from the vehicle. Her hands were twist-tied in front of her and she looked terrified.

"You're right here standing next to me in the next two minutes," Carrot-top said, "or my partner puts one in the back of your daughter's skull. I'm not kidding."

Something in the way the man spoke reminded Pruett of men he'd met in the war. The kind of men who weren't relieved when the war ended; the kind of men who immediately went looking for other work that suited their unique skills and desire to use them.

Agency men. Didn't matter which three-letter acronym. The only thing that *did* matter to Pruett was that men like that didn't know how to bluff.

"Coming down," Pruett said from the trees. He pressed send and pocketed the phone, never really knowing if the crucial text made it out or not. He placed his hands on top of his head without being asked. It took him a few minutes to pick his way down through the sagebrush, rocks, and ground scrub.

"Good man," Carrot-top said when Pruett reached him. "See, this whole thing can be done nice and organized. I sense you and I both appreciate organized, Sheriff."

"Fuck you," said Pruett.

Carrot-top clearly outranked his partner but he was too young to be the leader of the band. He said to his compatriot: "Zip-tie the sheriff. Nice and loose, no rough stuff. Just make sure he isn't getting those meaty paws free. And get me his gun." He kept the nine millimeter trained on Pruett's skull. The man knew cops wore standard issue Kevlar, even in the sticks.

The second man patted Pruett down, tossed his revolver to Carrot-top.

"The location is secure," Carrot-top said loudly to the SUV.

This time Agent Warren slipped out from the middle of the vehicle. Steam-pressed. Gray hair that didn't look premature but rather fabricated that way. A man who saw age not as a curse but an ally of time and knowledge and experience.

When he stood fully he was taller than Pruett, which Pruett had not noticed at their first meeting. Warren was more fit. The kind of man whose pounds were necessary—every one of them. When he walked toward the gathering his suit pants looked like they should crack with each step but instead were as silent as a cemetery. He stopped directly in front of Pruett, his face close enough for the sheriff to smell the bath soap the man had used that morning and the remnant lilt of a dissolved mint. The man smiled a smile that had cost him at least five figures.

"Sheriff," he said, looking as if he thought about extending a manicured hand and then didn't. The expression on his face said that he was a man who rarely touched other men even in the circumstance of polite tradition, much less strangers, or those men he saw as beneath himself. "Seems you were right. Things do indeed change."

"Imagine my elation. Wendy, you all right?" Pruett said, ignoring the Fed.

Wendy nodded. "But Jay…" she began.

"Smart of you to get bits of the evidence to the lawyer," Warren said. "Official document numbers; reference IDs, your friend in the Bureau. But we found him. He's waiting in town for us—alive, but only until we can verify he didn't have time to send the information elsewhere."

"Fucking cowards," Pruett breathed.

"Some don't think of us—of the BLM—well, they don't take us as seriously as some of the other government agencies. My predecessor," Warren continued, "would say things like 'well, we ain't the FBI, but we'll have to do, ma'am.' Or 'guess you were expecting the FeeBees. We'll do our best.'"

"Let my daughter go. She's got nothin' to do with this," Pruett said without confidence.

"She's got everything to do with it," Warren said. "Or else I wouldn't have her here."

"You're doing your agency proud at the moment," Pruett said.

"Things change as we get older, don't you think?" Warren said.

"Things change, all right," said Pruett. "But not the rules. Age doesn't give us a right to disavow our oaths, sir. That much I believe."

"I know your story," Warren said. "Happens I liked the fact you turned down that medal. If nothing else it embarrassed the Army something fierce. That's not why I liked the gesture, though. I had always hoped it was because you were more like me."

"Come again?"

"I thought you all should have been given a court-martial and put in prison for your collective treason."

"Treason?"

"I thought you might be thinking the same thing. That men who didn't follow orders didn't deserve medals. But that wasn't it. I knew the moment I looked in your eyes one afternoon on the television. One station or another was trying to get you to say something about your intentions, refusing such an honor."

"I never talked to anyone about my reasons," Pruett said. "Sure as hell ain't going to bring 'em up with you, here."

"I was there. In My Lai. We were fighting against barbarians, Sheriff, no different than the Romans in Carthage and Germania," Warren said. "Animals. We had our orders. We all did. You, too. Some of us followed them. Others took a different side."

"*You* were there?"

"First Battalion, Eleventh Brigade, just like you. But I followed my orders as my training prepared me to do. Don't worry, when this mess is discovered, the pieces put back together, I think most of your townsfolk will understand."

"Understand?"

"Why you went mad."

"All this for twenty million dollars," said Pruett. "All these lives. This community. Are *we* the enemy too, sir? Isn't this just treason for profit?"

"Twenty million? Is that what Tyree told you? For their properties, perhaps. Wyoming is a huge state. Several hundred million underground and everyone becomes the enemy."

"Then you are no less a traitor than anyone else," said Pruett.

"Maybe," said Warren. He looked at his men. "Get the rest of them out of the truck."

Cort and Honey climbed out of the vehicle of their own accord, son helping arthritic mother. It was always worse for her until she got moving. Ty was carried out by Carrot-top, manacled.

"So this is the plan," Pruett said. "Murder and robbing the good people of this state of their money. You make me sick. I was glad to stop your kind in 'Nam."

"*My kind*, was embattled, sir. We were killing the enemy."

"You were murdering then just as you're murdering now. Women. Children."

"Once a mind chooses to believe in the cause, age and gender are merely designations."

"I'm proud of my country," Pruett said. "Things like the Geneva Convention and rules of engagement. War tribunals. THAT is how we sort out the confusion. Is some eighteen-year-old German boy any more like Hitler than you or I or is *he* simply following orders? The jury and executioners are not humping gear out the jungle. We take prisoners. There are procedures."

"Perhaps we really are two different kinds of men," said Warren.

"I'm nothing like you," Pruett spat.

"You see women and children as something weaker, less capable of atrocity. I once witnessed a mother and daughter shred a Marine with a shoeshine box so horrifically there was nothing left with which his family could recognize him." He gestured to Honey as she stepped around the front of the SUV.

"War is Hell," said Pruett. "Ain't never been happy with it, not on either side."

"Your losses in this war are heavy."

"What?" Pruett said, his eyes narrowed and steady.

"In the way you lost your wife. I would think defending the woman who planned the whole ordeal would be impossible even for a man such as you."

Pruett looked over at Honey McIntyre, who was still too far away to hear the low voice of Warren.

"Shouldn't have happened," Pruett said. "Wrong place, bad timing."

"Say I could prove to you otherwise?"

"What do you mean?"

"Agent Higgins, give me the sheriff's revolver," Warren said to his man.

Higgins wiped the gun clean and handed it to his superior.

"The whole plan—everything—was coming together perfectly," Warren said. "But some people can't stop. True evil is like skin—it is the largest organ in the human body and eventually it controls everything, right down to the smallest of actions."

Special Agent Warren stepped up behind Honey McIntyre, who was looking at the trees, put the muzzle of Sheriff Pruett's revolver against the back of her skull, and pulled the trigger without a moment's hesitation.

"MOMMA," Ty cried out as Carrot-top attempted to subdue him, using the side of the vehicle, but had to call out for his partner and the both of them wrestled Ty all the way to the ground before the shackled man was in their control once again.

The rest of the participants stood still, like a diorama of a scene that had either just finished or was just beginning to play out. Cort McIntyre's eyes remained dreary and fixed on his boot tops the entire time.

Pruett kneeled, only because instinct and training told him he should. He stared at the fallen body of his mother-in-law, his face expressionless. So much had happened; the world for him was a place he no longer recognized as his own, nor even the same place he'd woken up in the day before.

When Honey went down it was more like she *lilted*; like a marionette when the strings that give it life are lowered and the play has ended. As she lay there, her tiny, arthritic hands and her other appendages half-pulled toward her in an awkward fetal position, Pruett was made to think of baby birds he'd seen as a child, the creatures having fallen from their nest, no doubt completely confused until the moment they hit the earth and died. Only Honey was dead before the echo of gunfire faded in the treed canyon beyond.

Pruett's eyes narrowed again and his facial muscles tightened in abhorrence. It mattered little now who stood for bad and who stood for good. The lines had become muddied and crisscrossed. They were—in one way or another—mostly murderers there.

The sheriff continued to stare at Honey for a moment longer, crumpled on the cold, hard earth. She no longer resembled an innocent bird to him but rather a decrepit carrion whose only purpose was to embrace death and sluice all the life it could from the living; eating and eating at the innocent until nothing remained but bone.

"The plan had always been to take out Rory," Warren said lowly and without so much as a tremor of remorse. "Only Honey and I knew the when and the where. We made sure Ty thought his old man tried to kill him, knew he'd come to the ranch to have it out."

"What in the hell happened?" Pruett hissed.

"I learned later, from Rance, that Honey sent her husband to the back of the house when she first heard the distant roar of her son's truck. She offered Bethy Rory's coat and hat and when Ty started yelling outside, she asked her daughter to please see if she could get her brother to calm down and come inside. Said to Bethy she'd have done it herself but that she had to check the boiling coffee."

"Why?" said Pruett, tears belying the iniquitous intent behind his stony eyes.

"I asked her," Warren said, pulling the sheriff to his feet. "Why the woman? She had no share of the parcels. She was an innocent in the proceedings. She said *that* was why. Innocence was the one thing she'd never been able to tolerate."

The Bull Rider's Prayer

As I live the Cowboy Way,
Protection is what I pray,
I don't know my Fate,
Outside of the gate.
If my ride sees trouble,
Send Angels on the double,
For in you the Lord I rest,
Let my life pass your test.
By pure grace I am saved,
Lord, ride with me,
That's the Cowboy Way,
And what bull riders pray.

Chapter 17

THERE WAS surely a time on Earth, maybe not even all that long ago, when there were places that evil had yet to find; places where greed and killing for no good reason at all—least of all *money*—still existed. Until a few weeks ago Sheriff James Pruett believed his town was one such place.

No longer. He understood the truth now. Evil was like water: it found the cracks and the weakest areas and the spaces the naked eye could not detect and it took them. It came. And there was no power more fierce and no flow that was stronger or more determined.

Corruption, torture, murder, family putting family in the ground— these were all just symptoms; signs that evil had run into a community and wasn't ever going to fully go away again. Or at least not the memory of what it accomplished.

Pruett was cuffed and leaning against the side of the Townsley cabin. The pair of corrupt federal underlings were busy working the forensics of the crime scene so that, when they had finished the day, it would all appear as Agent Warren wanted.

Cort was nearly catatonic. Ty had to be literally hogtied and gagged and lay with his back to the unfolding scene. Wendy sat next to her father, also gagged. Senior Agent Warren sat down next to Pruett, wiping the brittle leaves and dirt from his creased pants' legs and drawing his long legs up into a ninety degree bend, arms resting on his knees.

"I can almost *see* the lawman in you, figuring out the scene— guessing at how this will play out. I'd love to hear your take," Warren said.

"Fuck you. I'm not allowing you the pleasure."

"Nicely played, Sheriff. Well let me tell you what *your* town is going to find. They're going to find out that placing their confidence in you as their representative of law and order turned out to be wrong, like some of them probably thought all those years ago."

"Uh-huh."

"Honey, dead at your hand. Ty, hanged out of vengeance. Of course, after your rampage, you'll take the coward's way out."

"Cort lives," Pruett said. "You have to keep at least one family heir alive to funnel the money, right?"

"Things don't normally become as twisted as they did here in your fine county. The McIntyres proved to be a wily crew."

"What about my daughter?"

"I'm afraid you just couldn't bear to leave this world without her. As a lawman you know it's a common affair. Suicides many times take a loved one with them on their journey."

"Does your oath mean nothing to you, sir?" Pruett said.

"Garrison Keillor said: *Even in a time of elephantine vanity and greed, one never has to look far to see the campfires of gentle people.*"

"Meaning what?" said Pruett.

"Meaning—to me, anyway—that there are the elephants who rule their domain and there are the campfires of the gentle people who light their way."

"I'm pretty sure you got that one wrong."

"We bend the way of the world to our own design or we are run over by it as the scythe cuts down the grass. I admire a simple man such as yourself. Under a different time, a different circumstance, perhaps we could have been friends."

"I doubt that," said Pruett.

"As do I," Warren said, and stood, cleaning himself again.

Malcolm Whitefeather was a full-blooded Blackfoot. His grandparents were conquered by the United States Cavalry in the late eighteen-hundreds and rewarded with a small piece of dirt property on the reservation. His mother and father were born on the rez and died there, his father, too young—from a dead liver—and his mother at a respectable old age of eighty-two, still rocking her chair in the nine hundred square foot, federally-funded, manufactured home that Malcolm walked out of to join the Army one day after his eighteenth birthday.

The irony of Malcolm joining essentially the same Army that had warred against his people and stolen their land was not lost on him. However he'd always figured it was his only way off the rez and he'd decided when his father died and he was nearly convicted as a pyromaniac that he *would be leaving the rez.*

Whitefeather made it back from Vietnam so the Army had no choice but to educate him so that he could have a real job, away from the systemic, legalized imprisonment by the United States Government on the reservation. It didn't matter too much ultimately. By the time he got to the CBI mostly all he cared about was working with explosives. He did learn to care about being a lawman, too.

When Whitefeather retired and moved to be close to his friend James Pruett up in Wyoming country, he also decided to give back to his heritage by forming the Society of Blackfeet Warriors, a group of men aged seventeen to eighty-something who studied the old ways, met a few times a month to engage in activities from poetry readings to movie screenings. Once a year they did a live reenactment of a famous battle where the Blackfeet overcame an attack by the enemy, starved, outnumbered, and outgunned. Many of the younger members had served honorably in both Iraq and Afghanistan.

The gods of cell phone towers saw to it that Malcolm Whitefeather never received Sheriff James Pruett's final, desperate message, informing him the worst had come to pass.

He didn't have to.

By the time the band of seventeen Blackfeet rode down from the tree line, each with some symbolic swipe of war paint or carrying an ancestor's treasured shield or war bonnet but also armed with enough modern firepower to completely outgun Warren and his pair of stooges, the scene had nearly been staged and Pruett couldn't help but swell with love for his friend and admiration for his resolve and bravery.

A few minutes later Ty would have been swinging from the noose that Carrot-top had manufactured over a sturdy tree branch near the cabin. As it was, Ty had been placed atop a small picnic table that could be kicked from beneath his booted feet, the rope already placed around his neck.

Agent Warren and his men tried to defend their crumbling position and plan—*what other choice did they have?*, Pruett wondered—

but the fear the sheriff saw on their faces must've rivaled that of General George Armstrong Custer, his brother, Tom, and the rest of the 7th Cavalry as they faced down the insurmountable attack of Crazy Horse and White Bull and their forces of over three thousand Lakota-Sioux and Cheyenne.

As the mounted war party thundered down toward the cabin, Warren and his men returned fire and held their position fleetingly by retreating to the rear of the SUV. Whitefeather and his warriors knew, however, what was at stake, and they also knew that this was yet another attempt—albeit it now in the twenty-first century—by the federal government to steal from and kill innocents on land that had once been Native American territory.

The battle, therefore, did not last long. Pruett would never know whether Agent Warren fought bravely or cowered behind his men as the sheriff did not witness the dozen braves as they rounded the SUV and ended the fight, but in his mind he would always imagine the latter.

Whitefeather got to Pruett and Wendy first and cut their ties. Pruett embraced his daughter, holding her as though he'd never let her out of his protective grasp again.

Cort McIntyre had barely moved throughout the short onslaught, never brandishing a weapon and therefore escaping the wrath of the attackers. Pruett had seen men in the clutches of such terror, confusion, and outright helplessness before in war, and it sickened him to think how well the vision of the man trembling in place summed up the awfulness and disregard for human life represented by what had transpired there that afternoon.

Once freed and sure his daughter was fine, Pruett turned toward Ty, who was still standing, motionless, on the makeshift gallows created by his enemies. The cowpoke's head turned a few inches so that he could lock eyes with Pruett. What the sheriff saw in those eyes was the same look he'd seen at the trailhead after trying to kill Ty.

I should have let you, Ty's words reminded him.

And then Ty stepped off the table into the empty space below him.

"You won't need a reason
She don't let you choose
And so to make the game easy
Mother makes the rules"

Joe Walsh,
Mother Says

R.S. GUTHRIE

Chapter 18

LIVING WHERE you can see to what feels like the ends of the earth always filled Pruett with peace. He never could have survived in a jungle made of concrete—no easier, anyway, than he tolerated the jungles of Vietnam, where a man sometimes couldn't see past the end of his rifle. But in Wyoming, where the prairies still stretched out infinitely before a man, save for a small group of pronghorns he could feel as the Crow and the Blackfoot and the Sioux must have felt—as if men really did own the entirety of the Earth.

And Pruett knew, as the Native Americans knew—as his friend, Malcolm Whitefeather, who saved them all knew—when you owned something, you also owed it something. You owed it many things, actually, but respect perhaps more than anything. And Pruett respected the land. The land wasn't a vault for the greedy but a place for a person to build and live and grow, in harmony, with respect.

"I love you, Dad," Wendy Steele said as they sat side-by-side, leaning against the rails of the small Pruett cemetery where mother and wife Bethy rested—maybe in peace at last; now that the wrongs had been righted some.

His daughter's words—hearing them after all these years—almost made everything all right for Sheriff Pruett, too. In fact the words *did* make everything all right, at least for the moment, and Pruett was content to live there, in the now, and not to worry too hard on what might be coming next.

The mess the BLM and the McIntyre family laid out across the town of Wind River and the county of Sublette itself was grime that wouldn't be cleaned from the walls for some time, if ever. There was a poetic irony to the ending of the legalities, however: though patriarch Will McIntyre never considered a woman namely his granddaughter, Bethy—worthy of part or parcel when it came to family land and fortune, the probate court ruled that Cort's criminal conspiracy to obtain more than his share put him not only in prison but also in forfeiture of his part of the fortune. The court ruled to split the mineral royalties due on all McIntyre lands between the only two honest heirs, Bethy and Ty.

Bethy's share then went accordingly to her next living heir, Wendy.

Ty would be challenged not to drink away his small fortune, though he now had an entire ranch to run with no family and but a few rough hands to work for him.

Pruett never knew before but would now never forget that a true hangman's knot contains no fewer than thirteen coils, with the executioner placing the knot directly behind the left ear of the condemned. The design was meant to break the victim's neck, not strangulate him, which would be cruel and unusual. The young agent who manufactured *Ty's* noose made a simple slipknot, which would have still been more than effective at choking the life from the man.

When Pruett saw Ty step from the table at the Townsley cabin and the rope go stiff, he looked down to the ground and saw his revolver lying at his feet, where Warren had dropped it after murdering Honey McIntyre. The sheriff dropped to one knee, scooped up his sidearm, aimed at the highest point on the rope above Ty's head, let out half a breath to steady himself, and carefully squeezed off one round.

The bullet did not sever the rope but *did* split it in half—Ty's one hundred and seventy pounds was then enough to finish the job and the half-unconscious cowpoke dropped to the ground, breaking both ankles in the process.

Wendy and her father then hurried to where he lay, removed the rope, and verified the man's pulse and ragged but steady breathing.

"How's your uncle, Wendy?"

"You still haven't visited him?" she said.

Pruett shook his head and gazed off into the heavens. "Too hard. Too many mixed emotions still," he said. "Once a heart gives in fully to grieving, it's a process I guess. I'll be up to it one of these days."

"He's doing all right," Wendy said. "He's still drinking. But I think he's beginning to take to the idea that the McIntyre ranch and name are his to carry on."

"Like I said before, he ain't half bad."

Wendy pushed in closer to her father's side. "We're heading back to Laramie in the morning."

"You and the professor."

"Mm-hmm."

"No wedding bells yet? You wouldn't elope and rob me of a chance to walk you down the aisle now would you, girl?"

"Not yet. And no. When I walk down the aisle it'll be with the man I love most in the world by my side."

And in *that* moment Pruett just knew he could never feel happier again.

ABOUT THE AUTHOR

R.S. Guthrie lives in Colorado with his beautiful wife, three Australian Shepherds, and a Chihuahua who believes she's a forty-pound Aussie. The Guthrie dogs are their children and there is no disputing the fact that the canines rule the household.

The author's next planned book is the third in the Detective Bobby Mac series, but somewhere in the near future, there is a dog book digging to get out, and it will pay homage to the kindest, most loyal animals on the planet.

Pictured here with the author is three-year-old Elsa. She is as intelligent and as beautiful as she appears (and knows it all too well.)

Other books by **R.S.** Guthrie

<u>Sheriff James Pruett Mystery / Thrillers:</u>

Blood Land
Money Land
Honor Land

<u>Detective Bobby Mac Mystery / Thrillers:</u>

Black Beast
L O S T
Reckoning

<u>Non-Fiction:</u>

INK: Eight Rules To A Better Book

www.ingramcontent.com/pod-product-compliance
Lightning Source LLC
Chambersburg PA
CBHW060925120626
46557CB00003B/875